THE MURDER SUITE

THE AUDREY MURDERS

LEONIE MATEER

Published in the United States of America

Mystery/Crime/Fiction
Women's Fiction/Crime
10.02.2014

Paperback ISBN: 978-0-9908351–2-7
eBook ISBN: 978-0-9908351-0-3

For my sister, Pauline.
Who lovingly reads every word I write.

Chapter 1

Audrey tilted her glass and sucked the last few drops of wine as she reached for the bottle. At times she felt as though she had entered a hormonal fog that clung to every corner of her mind. The only clarity of thought was accompanied by a deep-seated anger. Everything made her angry.

Today she had plans. She had bookings in both chalets. One made by a man who enquired about local fishing spots and the other from a young couple on their honeymoon.

Remembering she had work to do she gulped the last of the wine, picked up the pile of freshly ironed linens and headed out into the bright sunshine.

Suite C was her favorite suite even though it was the smallest. It had a wonderful view across the rolling green farmland and out to the glistening blue waters of the bay. The room was spacious and airy. Marble tiles in the bathroom and terracotta tiles in the main room made it easy to keep clean. Audrey put fresh towels in the bathroom and stripped off the soiled bed linens replacing them with crisp clean sheets and covers. The morning sun soaked the native wood kitchen in a golden glow. Audrey polished the thick kauri bench top with concentrated dedication. She had created everything from the tropical gardens to the beautiful furnishings and transformed the old chalet style building into four-star plus luxury accommodation. Her guests came from every corner of the world. New Zealand was a tourist's dream vacation and her Chalets sat perched on a Maori pa overlooking one of the most beautiful places in the world.

Audrey kept busy. Busy stopped the dark from forming in her mind. Plenty of time for that, she thought as she placed fresh flowers in the chalets, a bottle of local wine in each fridge and a welcome note neatly on the native, wood crafted tables. When all her work was done Audrey went back to her suite and waited for the guests to arrive.

It wasn't long before she heard a car heading up to Suite A. It was the honeymoon couple. She made her way up the stairs to welcome them. They were so young. Audrey looked enviously as the young girl in short, shorts and small t-shirt. Her skin was bronzed and taut. Perfect red lips widened over white, straight teeth. The boy was obviously smitten by her. He carried the luggage from the car and they made their way inside. Audrey waited for the usual gasp of wonderment. She was not disappointed. There were not many suites like this one. 'Three levels of pure luxury" she called it on the website and it was. Audrey showed them how to work the fifty-inch widescreen TV and operate the hot tub on the deck. She wished them happiness during their stay and made her way back downstairs.

Then she saw him. He was pulling into the parking space in front of Suite C.

She immediately put him into balding, boring and bumptious category. He would be an easy target.

She waited until he had carried his luggage into the suite and made her way over to greet him.

Chapter 2

Doug had decided at the last minute to drive the four and a half hour's drive from Auckland to Whangaroa. His recent separation from wife number three had been expensive and painful. She had taken the house and he had taken a vacation. "Not fair" he mumbled under his breath. He had worked hard for that house and now he had to decide where he was going to live for the rest of his miserable life. All his belongings from his eight-year marriage fit into eight cardboard boxes. His golf clubs and his fishing poles now lived in the back of his truck along with everything else he owned.

His thoughts were drawn back to his first wife. That marriage had been his most successful only he hadn't realized it at the time. Work, work, work. That was all he thought about when he wasn't thinking about getting into some young girl's pants.

Those were the days. He visualized the evenings spent naked in their hot tub with neighbors and friends. They had even joined a nudist club but Doug didn't like the flabby old sods walking around eying his pretty wife. Wife swapping was the norm and hard liquor was preferred over wine.

Maybe he would get lucky on this fishing trip and he didn't mean fish. He looked down at his protruding stomach and ran his hand over his balding head. "I could lose a few pounds," he mumbled to himself. "This trip will do me good. A little exercise, fresh air, and freedom!"

Doug looked at the old map he kept in his side pocket of the door. He had already Googled the directions to the Three Suites but preferred the comfort of a real map. Only a few miles to go. He turned on the radio but there was too much static. *Who lives out here in the wop wops?* He wondered.

He saw the sign at the entrance and made a quick right turn up the long gravel driveway. Nice, he thought. Great view. He followed the sign to "Suite C" and pulled up at the "parking" sign. He stretched as he got out the car. His bones seemed to seize up when he sat for a long time and he had not taken a break since leaving Auckland. He made his way to the back of the truck and removed his bag.

It said on his reservation confirmation the key would be in the door. It was. He walked inside and was pleasantly surprised by the luxurious décor. He opened the glass doors and walked out onto the deck. A hot tub

sat in the corner making a welcoming hum.

He sat at the small round wood table and took a deep breath. This is just what I need, he thought. Then he heard her. The cheery, "Welcome" was followed by the sight of a buxom, blonde woman in huge sunglasses and the biggest breasts he had ever set eyes on.

"Hello," he replied.

"Just wanted to welcome you and show you how to use the spa," she said as she lifted up the spa cover and pointed to the controls. "If it makes too much noise when you go to bed, just turn it off and restart it in the morning. There is a complimentary bottle of wine in the fridge for your enjoyment," she added with a smile.

"Wonderful. Say, would you like to join me for a glass?" he asked wondering what the hell he was doing.

"That would be nice," she beamed. He made a move. "Don't get up, I'll get it," she said as she made her way inside to collect the wine and a couple of glasses.

They sat outside and admired the view and chatted aimlessly about the area. Audrey gave directions on where to find the best fishing spots, where the nearest shop was located and what local restaurants served the best food.

"Have you been here before?" asked Audrey.

"No, never," he replied. "I have always wanted to see the far north and decided it was time to take some time off and check out the fishing. I might even play a round of golf while I am here."

"Do you know anyone up this way?"

"Not a soul. In fact, everything I own is in the back of my truck and I might just decide to stay a while up here. Find a house to rent and spend the summer." Doug looked out into the distance at the sparkling waters and began to like what this place was doing to him. Deep in thought he didn't notice the strange flicker of a smile that wiped curiously across Audrey's red lips.

Chapter 3

Audrey returned to her suite and turned on the television. She lay back on her bed and flicked across the channels trying to find something of interest. Her mind was on the guest in Suite C. She had left him to unpack and enjoy the evening. She found conversations with strangers exhausting. Thank goodness she just had to welcome the guests and check them out when they left. Easy really. All the suites were self-contained so she didn't have to provide meals or daily cleaning services. Often the guests would invite her in for a drink and sometimes they even invited her to join them for a meal. Mostly she hid in her suite with the curtains drawn hoping they would not enter her solitary world. The guests mistakenly thought she was a social creature because she could converse with such confidence. The reality was, Audrey was a recluse, locked in her own private hell of self-incriminations and regrets.

Finding nothing to watch on TV, Audrey decided to have a shower and clean herself up for an evening of possibilities.

She knew Doug's type. He would either call her or knock at her door when the sun was setting and invite her over for a drink and a spa. It was always the same. Men like him didn't like to be alone. She presumed he was just getting out of a relationship. His sort didn't wander around the country with their life's possessions in tow without a good reason. His booking was for two nights so she had plenty of time. She would take it slowly. Everything needed to go to plan.

Careful to cover her tracks, Audrey had accessed the information she needed from the Internet café in Kerikeri - thirty miles away. It had taken weeks of planning and research. She laughed out loud when she read: The difference between fun and fucked up, when taking G, is less than a teaspoon. It was perfect!

Deciding to use GHB was easy. It was available, illegally of course. Already diluted in clear water and with only a slightly salty taste it was easy to disguise in a glass of wine. Of course, taking GHB with alcohol or sedatives could cause immediate death. Oh Damn. And taking more than the suggested 1-3 gram recreational dose is also fatal. Damn again.

It could take as little as five minutes to begin taking effect and the effects could last up to three hours.

Plenty of time to put her plan into action.

Chapter 4

Police Constable Driver was still at work. He had only been at the station a week and was looking forward to his family joining him in a couple of days. He hoped his wife of thirteen years would like it here. The local station had an adjoining three-bedroom, weatherboard bungalow, which was one of the reasons he took this position in the middle of nowhere.

The small town of Kaeo had a population of just over five hundred residents that grew considerably during the tourist season due mainly to the enticement of the nearby Whangaroa Harbor, known as New Zealand's game-fishing capital.

The tourists, he was told, did not cause many problems. It was the drugs. Northland was known for its marijuana crops hidden among the native bush. But recently the biggest problem was P. It had become an epidemic and was creating a growing problem. P houses spotted the deserted farmlands well known by locals but conveniently concealed to tourists.

The Maori population in the far north was substantial.

Maori and Pacific Islanders made up the majority of modern day gangs such as Black Power, Hells Angels, Mongrel Mob and Nomads. Driver knew New Zealand had seventy major gangs – more gangs per head than any other country in the world. Having already read up on the gang activities in the area he felt that he was adequately prepared. At least he hoped he was.

Police Constable Driver knew he had taken on a big task. Even though the population was small he recognized there was unrest here. His predecessor left because he had been badly beaten with his own batten by a local gang member. Which was both embarrassing and violent. Driver knew that the same could happen to him. Local policemen didn't carry guns and Tasers had just been introduced. He would need to be on alert at all times.

He looked up at the big-breasted blonde tapping her fingernails on the counter. He had not heard her come in. "Can I help you?" he asked.

"Yes, she said. "I need you to contact the FBI. I am getting phone calls from some lottery company who insists I have won millions. They are calling me at home. It's scary. They know my name. I thought it was for real at first and then realized they were just a con. Can you do something about it? They are scamming single women living alone in New Zealand – it needs to stop". Her green eyes were cold and demanding as she just stood there waiting for his response.

"We don't have an FBI in New Zealand," Driver responded. "We have Interpol but I don't think they can do much in this circumstance." The blonde looked frustrated. "I have only been here a couple of days." He didn't know why he confided this to her. Maybe it was because he couldn't help anyway, and it seemed a way to soften to blow.

"Oh, welcome to Kaeo. I hope you will be happy here." She tucked a few loose strands of blonde hair into her stubby, short ponytail and left.

Strange, thought Driver. He breathed a heavy sigh and returned to his paperwork.

Chapter 5

Audrey slammed the door as she entered her suite. She had run down to the local grocery store to pick up some more wine, cheese and biscuits in the event she would be entertaining tonight. She had stopped by the local police station while she was there. For the past two nights she had not been able to sleep thinking about how her life will change now she had won eight hundred thousand British pounds in an online lottery. She had explained to the man who telephoned with congratulations she had not entered any lottery competition. He had immediately explained her website had been chosen at random and, in fact, she was indeed a winner.

It wasn't until this morning, after numerous convincing telephone calls from the lottery' organizers, she had reluctantly given him her bank information to deposit the money. Then with horror she realized that it could all be a con. Research online had proven it to be a fact. She was so disappointed and angry she had been "taken in." She had felt her anger rising to new levels when she realized the new policeman would not help her and they would get away with it. She would need to call the bank on

Monday morning and confess her stupidity and have them close her account and open a new one. Bloody life! Nothing was easy. One minute you think you are going to live free of debit for ever and the next minute you realize that life is just shit after all.

She placed the wine and cheese in the fridge and the biscuits on the counter top and turned as she heard a knock at her door. It was the man. She knew it would be. Predictable they were. She opened the door and saw him standing there with his laptop in his hand.

"I cannot seem to get the wireless Internet to work," he said.

"Maybe if you try logging on again here," Audrey said pointing to the outside table on her patio. "Then, once connected, it should work in your suite. It happens sometimes." She waited while he reconnected.

"It works," he said relieved and started back towards Suite C.

"Great," Audrey said and returned back inside. Well, I was wrong, she thought. He didn't invite me back. She opened up the fridge and removed a fresh bottle of wine. Audrey liked how New Zealand wines had screw caps on the wine bottles. Even the better wines had screw caps. Made it easier to open and you could replace the cap, unlike a swollen cork. She poured a half glass and returned the bottle to the fridge. She made a plate of cheese and biscuits, sat on the sofa and turned on the telly. It was going to be quiet night after all.

Chapter 6

Doug checked his email. Maybe there was a message from his wife asking him to come back saying it was all a mistake or from one of his daughters. He only visited his daughters once or twice a year. Both lived in Queenstown where he and his first wife had lived. They had never left the idyllic town and now worked in the tourism business promoting the local ski fields. The sisters were best of friends but were closer to their Mother than to him. They always blamed him for the divorce so many years ago. He looked at the screen. Just the usual junk mail and a couple of emails from the guys at work. He didn't feel like responding so he logged out and put the computer away. A soak in the hot tub and a nice dinner would raise his spirits and get him ready for a day on the water.

Doug walked into the huge closet and removed his clothes. He donned the complimentary robe hanging on the wooden coat hanger. He liked this suite. It wasn't too fussy, not like the bed and breakfast places his wives like to stay in. They had fancy bedspreads and frilly curtains and he hated having to talk to the owners in the communal TV lounges. Horrible. He liked his privacy.

But he did miss female company. He had considered hiring a professional for a few hours. But the nearest brothel was in Whangarei almost two hours away. Legalizing prostitution in New Zealand in 2003 was a marvelous thing as far as Doug was concerned. A few hundred dollars got him everything he would ever want from a woman, less the nagging. It was perfect. Unfortunately his last wife had not taken kindly to his costly pastime. Now he was free to do what he wanted, when he wanted. But tonight he would have to do without. Then his mind wandered to the blonde woman owner. She was a little heavy for his liking and a little old but she had great tits and nice legs. After four or five drinks she would look even better.

Doug poured himself another glass from the wine bottle. He would pop over and ask her if she would like to join him in the hot tub over a glass of wine. After all, this was the boondocks and he couldn't be too particular. Too much trouble, he thought. I will ring her, and he picked up the phone and dialed the office number.

Chapter 7

She answered the phone "Good evening, Three Suites."

"Would you like to join me for a glass of wine and watch the sunset from the hot tub? This is Doug in Suite C."

Audrey smiled. Now, that was more like it, she thought. "OK," she said "I will change and join you in a minute or two." She hung up the phone and walked upstairs to her bedroom and chose a simple black suit. No suit could disguise her large breasts. She slipped into a matching black wrap to cover her body as best she could and made her way across the terracotta-colored courtyard to the deck of Suite C.

He was waiting at the table in his bathrobe, drinking wine and looking at the sun setting over the water. Colors of orange, reds and yellows adorned the horizon. The few clouds captured the colors and rays of light reflected their warm glow onto the surrounding landscape. It was breathtaking.

Audrey almost forgot she was angry and disillusioned with life as she sat quietly beside the man in the calm evening light.

As the last of the sun disappeared below the hills in the

distance Audrey stood and switched on the deck lights. Doug removed the lid from the hot tub and Audrey stepped into the warm, scented water lowering herself gingerly until only her head and shoulders were exposed to the cool evening air. She watched as Doug removed his robe and then it happened. All the anger she had been feeling for the past few days exploded in her mind. She closed her eyes to hide the monster building inside her. Doug stepped into the tub. His soft, flabby penis hung shamelessly between his legs. His protruding belly was covered in dark curly hairs that matched his pubic hairs. Naked! Always naked, thought Audrey. Why do these men have no decorum, no shame? They flaunt their manhood as though it is a winning lottery ticket. Don't men know that nakedness is not attractive over fifty – unless they have the body of younger man?

Audrey blamed legalized prostitution for the way men behaved today. They actually believed pretty prostitutes when they told them they were handsome and virile. The women took global vacations on money they took from stupid men.

A few months ago, an owner of a chain of brothels had stayed in Suite A. Audrey had been fascinated by her chosen profession and asked. "How many women actually liked having sex with strangers? The owner had confessed that in her twenty years of running brothels in New Zealand only one woman had ever admitted she actually enjoyed her profession. "The women do it for the money," she had said. "Nothing else."

Audrey knew that New Zealand men didn't date. Not like American men did. They preferred a sure thing and a prostitute was a sure thing without any complications. Married men, single men, it didn't matter. Prostitution gave them what they wanted. Sadly New Zealand women suffered the consequences. Romance didn't exist and chivalry went out with the prehistoric moa.

Audrey realized that Doug was talking. At least his mouth

was moving and she strained to hear him over the loud hum of the jets. She kept her eyes level with his. Not daring to look down in case she glimpsed his soft penis bobbing in the clear blue bubbles. How Audrey hated penises. If only she could be gay then penises would not be an issue. She decided to get out of the hot tub and return to her suite. Tonight was not the right time for what she had in mind - maybe tomorrow night? She said that she had work to do, grabbed her towel and wrap and walked barefoot across the courtyard to the comfort and privacy of her suite.

Chapter 8

What is her problem? One minute she is sitting happily at the table watching the sunset and the next minute it was like she saw a ghost. Bloody women! You can't live with them and you can't live without them.

Doug climbed out of the hot tub, had a shower, dressed and drove his truck down to the local waterfront restaurant. He noticed how dark it was in the country. The sky was a landscape in itself. The Milky Way was breathtaking. The Southern Cross was easily recognizable. Doug had never seen such a night sky before. This truly was a piece of paradise. He decided to eat outside to enjoy the evening air and the vastness of the evening. He could hear morepork owls in the distance. Their cry "more pork! more pork!" Gave them their well-earned name. It was a loud call for a reasonably small owl. Their yellow round eyes watched for flying bugs attracted by porch lights of neighboring houses.

He had ordered fish and chips and was pleasantly surprised at the freshness of the fish. New Zealanders knew that if you could smell the fish then it wasn't fresh – the same with meat. Farmers cannot stand the smell in a butcher shop. "Rotting meat," they would say. "Fresh meat does not smell".

Doug was interested in the local farming. New Zealand used to have over seventy million sheep. Now, due to strong international demand, there are seven million dairy cattle, four million beef cattle and a marked reduction in sheep numbers to thirty million. Most beef farms were in the North Island and Doug noticed during his drive up north many of the farms were now cattle farms with just a few sheep added to the mix.

He liked this area. Seemed like a good group of guys in the Club. Mostly standing around tall tables drinking beer and discussing the weather, as most farmers did. "Looks like a long dry summer," He heard a rugged faced, tall skinny guy announce as he ordered another beer. "Hope the grass holds out".

Doug drank his second beer and decided to head on back to the Chalets. It was getting a little chilly and the hot tub would be just the ticket. He might even get blondie to take another dip. No women in the bar. He glanced at the pub across the street. It, too, was full of men. Most of them spilled outside smoking cigarettes and clutching a beer - their voices rowdy and raucous in the still night air.

Chapter 9

Constable Driver headed out into the dark night to check on things. All seemed pretty quiet. A couple of burglaries were reported on Wainui Road not far from the fishing club. He would check out the area to see if anyone was acting out of the norm. He drove the eight miles down to the waterfront turnoff. He liked Whangaroa Harbor. He had heard that it was a main tourist spot years ago. The tourist buses used to stop there. Now the buses missed the turnoff and drove straight up the ten highway to Manganui where they stopped for fish and chips on their way to the northern tip of Cape Reinga. There they could see the joining of both the Pacific Ocean and the Tasman Sea. Now Whangaroa Harbor just had its docks, a small club restaurant, a bar, a few local residents, a couple of motels and a dairy. The docks were pretty full of local boats. Further down the road there was an old jetty and a boat ramp. Locals fished for kahawai, terakihi, trevally, and snapper off the dock.

Driver pulled into the fishing club car park and noticed a guy getting into his truck. He didn't recognize him as one of the locals but it was dark and he couldn't be sure. The truck was a black Toyota with heavy tires. It didn't look like a farmer's truck, it was much too tidy. Looked as though it belonged to city-type guy. Most likely up here for the fishing. Driver decided to go back to the fork in the road and make sure that the locals were not driving over the legal limit. He had found a spot at the Wainui Road turnoff where he could watch the traffic in three different directions. Everything seemed pretty quiet, it was going to be a long night, but he had no one to go home to. At least not until his family arrived. As he parked the car and reached over to grab the coffee thermos and the sandwiches he had packed for his dinner, he noticed the black Toyota heading up Wainui Road towards Tauranga Bay. Not much up there, thought Driver - just the chalets and a few rental cabins at the bay. He watched the truck taillights disappear around a curve in the road. All fell quiet again.

Pearl looked out her window at the cop car parked across the road. She made a quick call to the restaurant and the pub to warn them that the new Constable was on the prowl. She promised to call again when he left. She smiled at his naivety. Sometimes the paddy wagon parked there in order to stop all the cars going in and out of the harbor, hoping to catch the boozers on a Saturday night. Pearl always warned the pubs, and the cops wondered why the traffic suddenly became non-existent. Tonight would be the same. *Shame really*, Pearl thought. *He seems like a nice young cop.*

Pearl knew everything that went on in the little Whangaroa Township. Her cozy, buttercup yellow, one bedroom cottage was neatly fringed with a well- tendered garden of hollyhocks, flowering bushes, bromeliads, and succulents galore. Pearl loved her garden. A little wooden gate led to her front door. She would sit on her patio and watch the locals come and go. If there was a stranger in town, Pearl knew about it.

She had just seen a strange black truck head off up Wainui Road. It was too dark to see who was driving it but she did know he wasn't from around here. Pearl returned to her knitting. She was making scarves for the library gift shop in town. She liked to keep busy.

Twenty minutes later she heard the police car start up and drive off towards town. She called the pubs to give the all clear. A few minutes later she heard the traffic began to flow.

Chapter 10

Audrey looked at the time. It was ten o'clock. She heard his truck coming up the driveway. She peeked through her curtains as the man turned off the lights, got out of the truck and headed inside Suite C. *Guess he just went down to the waterfront restaurant,* she thought. Audrey went there some nights when they had their roast dinner menu. The locals knew they could get a good feed for only twenty dollars. Trouble was, you couldn't go back for seconds. It was a help yourself type arrangement and every now and then a stranger would confuse the set up with a smorgasbord and think it was "all you could eat" and would go back for seconds only to be instantly and curtly scolded for his ignorance. A good crowd would turn out. Tonight was Saturday night and she knew that the restaurant and the pub would just be full of the local drinking crowd, mostly men.

Whangaroa was an older community with the average age of the residents fifty, even sixty and older.

She hadn't heard a peek out of the honeymoon couple upstairs. They were checking out tomorrow and as she had no-one checking into the suite for a couple of days, she didn't have to rush around cleaning it tomorrow. It could wait. She had too much on her mind at the moment. She needed a plan.

Audrey had done her research and had been planning this for months. She just had to wait until the right time and place. She was a believer that life was all about luck and timing. Be it bad luck or good luck, it didn't seem to matter. It was the timing that was most important. Tomorrow night would be the perfect time. It would only be her and the man here. Her twelve acres of complete privacy gave her all the cover she would need.

She walked over to the door and turned out all the lights. He would think she had gone to bed and not disturb her tonight. Tomorrow he would head off early to get in a full day's fishing. Audrey stripped off her clothes and hopped into her king size bed naked. She liked the feel of the cool crisp sheets against her body. She also liked sleeping alone. So many years of living a single life had spoiled any possible relationship she might now have. The sound of an old man snoring beside her was repulsive, irritating and sleep depriving. In her youth she never seemed to notice snoring. She thought it was because she always fell asleep first or maybe it simply didn't matter then. She turned on her telly quietly so that no one would hear it if they came to her door. She usually went to sleep with the telly on and the sleep mode set for forty-five minutes.

The pa was busy tonight. An off-sea wind muffled grunts and squeals from deep in the pine forest.

Chapter 11

Audrey awoke to the sound of his truck crunching down the gravel driveway. It was only seven o'clock. She rolled over and went back to sleep for another hour. When she finally awoke bright sunshine was streaking through the curtain gaps into her bedroom. Feeling hungry, she walked downstairs to the kitchen and turned on the jug for a cup of tea and popped a piece of bread into the toaster. She could hear movements in Suite A and returned to her bedroom quickly throwing on her jeans and t-shirt and twisting her hair into a ponytail. In the bathroom she splashed cold water on her face.

"Shit, I look awful," she confined to her reflection in the mirror. Any minute she expected the young boy to knock at her door so she could check them out. They must be leaving early, she thought. The toaster popped out the toast and the jug stopped boiling.

Audrey didn't like mornings. She awoke feeling headachy and sore all over and lived on painkillers. It was a habit to reach for her pills the minute she woke, popping two into her hand and taking a gulp of water to swill them down.

She blamed her headaches on her bra straps digging into her shoulders and causing the constant neck pain radiating up the back of her head. She had weighed her boobs by putting the scales on the kitchen table and placing her boobs on the scale. Forty-five pounds they weighed! Twenty-two and a half pound each! No wonder she had a constant headache.

Audrey was right. The young boy, all fresh faced and fanciful was knocking at the door downstairs. She welcomed him inside, took his credit card and ran it through the machine.

"I hope you enjoyed your stay," she said as she printed out his receipt, stapled it to his bill and handed him the copies.

"Thanks," he said. "It was great. We are heading off to Cape Reinga today. How long do you think it will take?" he asked.

"It will take you about an hour and a quarter to get to the east coast from here and another couple of hours to the top. But you should stop on the way and visit the white silicone beaches. You can drive legally on ninety mile beach and the sand dunes are great for boogie boarding," she offered.

"We will," he said as he left. "We left the keys on the kitchen counter."

"Thanks, goodbye," she called back as he headed up the steps.

Alone at last, she thought. As soon as she heard their car driving away, she made her way upstairs. Might as well do the linens and laundry she thought as she stripped the super king bed. Everything got washed and ironed. She took armfuls of bed linens and towels down to the laundry and started the first load then made her way upstairs again to make the bed and clean the kitchen. You never knew when someone just might drop by to enquire about a vacancy. Today, however, she would not put up the vacancy sign at the gate. Tonight she wanted privacy - just her and the man.

The day was taken up with cleaning, washing, ironing and changing the water in the hot tub upstairs. She took pride in keeping the hot tubs clean and inviting. No one wanted to bathe in the same water as the honeymoon couple the night before. Each suite had it's own private hot tub which was one of the major attractions of her business.

Audrey had spent a fortune on her tropical gardens. Thick luscious palm trees bordered the driveways, shading hundreds of healthy succulents and native ferns.

The gardens reminded her of the gardens in Montecito, California where she had lived for many years before returning to live in New Zealand. The locals thought she was a rich American when she moved into their town. She wasn't. She had spent every penny she had ever earned and even borrowed more to create this masterpiece. The business was all she had. Originally she had lived in the South Island which might as well have been a different country from the far north. This was something else. It was hard to relate to the locals whose lives had been spent living off the land. Audrey's life had been spent living off her wits. She had very little education but had been moderately successful using her youth, femininity, intuition and common sense to get her through. Her youth was now behind her and her femininity had only just got her into trouble. Men had been her Achilles heel since day one. Audrey blamed everything that ever went wrong with her life on men. Her Father, her two husbands, her countless lovers, they had all let her down. Now it was time for men to pay. Tonight would be the beginning of her next project and Audrey knew she wasn't happy if she didn't have a project.

Chapter 12

Doug was feeling quite contented. He had found a great fishing spot and had settled down for a day of fishing and some serious beer drinking. He had stopped at the little grocery store in Kaeo before heading off and picked up some bait and a supply of beer.

It was a great little store, he thought. Had a good selection of beer and wine, which was surprising for a little store in the middle of nowhere. He also grabbed some bread, ham and cheese and a couple of packets of potato chips. The sun was out and the day had nice breeze: all good. Catching a couple of snapper he knew dinner was set. Maybe he would invite the blonde, Audrey, over for dinner. Would be nice to have some company and perhaps he would get lucky. He grinned. Being single again is not such a bad deal. He might even stop over in Whangarei on the way back to Auckland and get himself a girl or two. He had been checking out the girls' online last night. Some pretty tasty girls; young Maori girls, Asian girls, Pakehas with big tits - quite a selection.

His line jerked and broke him out of his fantasy. A "big one" this time. Doug couldn't remember the last time the fish had been so kind to him. He twisted the large snapper off the hook and placed it on the chopping board. It was a good size and provided a couple nice big fillets of which he put in the chilly bin. He scraped off the board and threw all the remnants into the ocean. Doug fished and drank beer all morning, ate his lunch and continued to do the same through the afternoon. By the time he decided to head back to his chalet he had a full chilly bin of filleted fish and a full stomach of beer. He didn't have to drive far to get back and he knew that cops were few and far between out here in the far north so he had no worries about being stopped.

Chapter 13

Constable Driver was worried. He hadn't heard from his wife all day. She was supposed to be doing the final packing up of their house in Auckland and he knew it was a big job and he was sure that she would call him to complain that it was just too much.

She had not been well the past few years. Her illness had caused a problem for him at his last job and he hoped the new therapy was helping. He wondered how the boys would take to their new home and school here in Kaeo. He had considered sending the boys to Kerikeri for school but it meant taking the bus in and out every day and he hoped he could support the local school even though the school's academic reputation was poor. Most of the kids in the area went to Kerikeri. He would leave the decision up to his wife. He had hired a local lady to prepare the house for their arrival. She had washed all the curtains, scrubbed the floors and made all the beds with clean linens. Everything else was to arrive with the family on Monday. There were just a few days to go.

Driver considered eating a roast dinner at Whangaroa

tonight. He had heard that it was good tucker and he needed a home cooked meal. Roast lamb, roast pork and roast beef with roasted potatoes, kumara, pumpkin, cauliflower with cheese sauce and peas and gravy. His mouth watered just thinking about it. He would head over there early and do a sweep of the area while he was at it. It wouldn't hurt to get to know some of the locals.

The phone rang. It was his wife. He breathed a sigh of relief. She sounded happy and excited. The packing was done. The truck was organized for tomorrow. It would arrive in Kaeo at noon on Monday. She and the boys would drive up Monday morning and be there in time to help unpack. She said the boys were really excited and they were looking forward to kayaking and fishing. Driver had promised that he would buy them both kayaks so they could go out in the harbor and up the Wainui River when the tide was in. They were ten and eleven years old and good swimmers so he had no fear of them being around water.

He felt relieved that his wife was coping with the move. He hung up the phone, donned his jacket, grabbed his hat and headed off out the door. He had work to do and he wanted to get to the dinner tonight. He heard the local roast pork was truly delicious.

CHAPTER 14

Audrey was prepared and excited. *Finally*, she thought. *This is the right time*. She had been feeding the wild pigs for a couple of months now. Always in the same place so they would expect to find the food there. She had learned about pigs from the local pig farmer. He had told her that if a man falls down in a pigpen and can't get up the pigs would eat him alive. She had always been afraid of pigs since then. Once when helping a neighbor head off a straying calf she realized she was alone in a muddy paddock surrounded by huge pink menacing sows. As they headed towards her she ran as fast as she could, terrified she would fall and they would attack her.

She knew she had chosen the perfect spot. It was in a small valley in the forest that surrounding the chalets. It was an isolated spot off the beaten track. She had set up a makeshift pigpen where she would toss pieces of raw meat. The wild pigs would come down from the hills at dusk and feed then return up into the hills at night. Audrey had counted four wild black pigs. Everyday she hoped that the local farmers would not shoot them.

Pig hunting was not only a favorite pastime for farmers, but also a necessity, as their constant rooting made a mess of the paddocks.

Pigs had to be some of the most awful animals on earth, thought Audrey. *Pigs and men*! She had heard that some mother pigs even ate their own piglets. Disgusting! She had chosen the dumping site because she could drive her Rav4 and trailer right up to the pen. Audrey had planned everything carefully and she wasn't going to rush things and make any mistakes. If tonight was going to be the night then she would make sure that everything was perfect.

Audrey had just taken a hot tub with a glass of wine and was still in her robe. She hadn't decided what to wear tonight. Something soft, feminine and alluring she had decided. Her hair was up in big rollers. She chose a long flowing blue skirt and matching blue top with a scarf wrapped around her hips. The scarf took the emphasis away from her breasts and seemed to balance her out. Her pretty sandals with a wedge heel would add height to her five foot four frame. Finally she brushed out her blonde hair and tied it back with a curled hairpiece. She almost looked pretty once her make up was applied.

Would I be pretty enough to do what I need to do? she wondered.

Chapter 15

Doug made it back to his chalet without being caught by a cop. He hadn't realized just how much he had drunk until he started driving down the country gravel roads. Twice he had skidded and almost slipped over the edge. "Shit!" he cursed as he wondered if the chilly bin was still intact and hoping the fish had not spilled into the back of his truck. He would never get the smell out if the mess had soaked into his cardboard boxes. He finally arrived at The Three Suites and made it up the driveway. As he staggered out of the truck he looked around to make sure that blondie was not around. Not good for her to see him in this condition. He needed to sober up a bit before he invited her to dinner. Maybe she would cook the fish for them. "Women," he cursed. "All they are really good for is humping and cooking." He felt in his pants pocket for the key and opened the door. Once inside he kicked off his boots and collapsed facedown on the bed and fell fast asleep.

He heard a soft knocking on the glass door. He felt like shit.

"Who is it?" he shouted back.

"It's me, Audrey."

"Bugger!" he muttered. "Just a minute!" he shouted back. He looked at the clock and saw he had been asleep for over an hour. He walked into the bathroom and splashed cold water on his face and over his balding head. He patted down the sides and wiped his face and headed for the door. "What is it?" he asked, as he opened it.

"I just wondered if you needed anything," she said.

He noticed that she was all dolled up. "Going somewhere?" he asked.

"I thought I might pop down for the roast dinner at the club," she said. "Tonight is roast dinner night and you won't find a better meal anywhere else around."

Doug thought about the fish in the back of the truck and the last thing he felt like doing was cooking it. "I just have to pop my catch in the freezer," he explained "and take a shower. I'll meet you down there. What time does it close?"

"Eight o'clock," she said. "Or earlier. Depends on the crowd. Sometimes they run out of food by seven o'clock and have to close the restaurant. Best to get there as soon as you can." And with that she spun on her heels and headed off in the direction of her parked car.

Doug watched her drive away down the long gravel driveway then walked back into the bathroom and ran the shower. So far, so good. It looked as though things were going nicely to plan. A nice meal, a few drinks and, to top it off, a big buxom blonde all to myself. He even whistled in the shower. *This holiday was a good idea*, he thought as he pulled on his jeans, grabbed a clean shirt, and donned his best boots. He was becoming a regular down at the waterfront and looked forward to a nice roast lamb dinner. They may even serve roast pork, his favorite.

CHAPTER 16

They were all there, the locals. Pearl was dressed in her favorite outfit resembling a bright blue and yellow butterfly with huge matching beads and earrings. She was a tall, slender, woman who liked to look her best. Everyone knew Pearl. She had lived in Whangaroa for many years and was born in Kaeo - came from a farming family and spent many years milking cows and tending chickens. Her retirement to the little house on the corner was all she ever wanted. Tonight she was sitting with other locals enjoying the local gossip.

They looked up as the local constable from Kaeo walked in. He was out of uniform apparently taking the night off. He looked a little shy and reserved. A few of the local farmers nodded at him and the constable walked over to greet them. Pearl was dying to meet him. He was such a good-looking man. She had heard his wife and boys were going to move into the police house this week. She was pleased for him. He must be missing his family and this is not really a young town.

She looked over at the door and saw the lady from The Three Suites entering. She knew her name was Audrey and kept pretty much to herself. She didn't appear to have any friends around here and had been living there for a few years now. Pearl had heard the local men talking about her. "More money, than sense" they would say. Everyone wondered where she got her money. They heard she had lived in America for some time, and they knew her family was not from around here. She had a reputation of being a hard worker and, in most people's eyes, that was a compliment.

"Too many lazies living off the dole around here," the farmers would moan.

She watched as the lady chose an empty table and then went to the bar and ordered a drink. She returned and sat quietly sipping her wine and looking at the door. *Was she waiting for someone*? Pearl wondered with curiosity. *I wonder whom*?

The men in bar were watching sport on a big screen TV hung high in the corner of the bar. They were cheering and cursing. Pearl didn't watch much sport and had no idea what game they were watching. Dinner was served in the big room attached to the bar. There were glass doors leading out onto a patio looking out across the docks on the harbor. Big fishing boats were anchored for the night. Dozens of private boats were docked neatly in rows. The last of the day's weary fishermen were carrying heavy chilly bins down the dock towards their trucks.

The restaurant was crowded both inside and out. It was a good night for the cooks who rented the space and who really only made a profit on the Special Roast Dinner nights.

Pearl saw him enter through the main bar door. He was a balding man in his late fifties. Nicely dressed in pressed jeans and jacket. Must be from the big city, she thought. He went up to the bar and walked away with a beer. He looked around and headed for the restaurant.

She watched as Audrey waved to him. So that is whom she is

waiting for, Pearl thought. I wonder if he is a guest at her chalets or if he is her boyfriend? She got her answer pretty quickly when she saw how awkwardly they greeted each other. *A guest*, thought Pearl. *Has to be*. And went back to listening to the local gossip and enjoying her meal.

She couldn't help but keep an eye on the strange couple during the evening. She couldn't quite make out what vibe she was getting from Audrey. The man obviously was ready for anything. He had a red face as if he was quite a drinker - but also a gentleman, always standing when Audrey stood and held her chair for her. Real city manners. She wished the locals treated a lady that well.

The average age in the restaurant must have been fifty-five. It would have been sixty-five but there were a few younger couples, obviously boaties, who had stopped off for a meal. A few kids ran around outside. It was a nice area with an adjoining green park and park benches strategically positioned so one could sit and look out over the harbor.

It was a leisurely five-minute walk down the windy, one-way, gravel road to the pier. The road stopped at the big house at the end with a sign "private road" preventing further access. Big pahutekawa trees hung over the roadway and clung tenaciously to the bank. Houses lined the narrow road on one side. Every little cottage was unique in style and color. New Zealanders liked to paint their houses in an array of colors especially the Maoris. Bright teals, blues, greens and yellows created a spectacle of color. Whangaroa was no different. Many houses throughout Northland were holiday baches converted into retirement homes.

Pearl and her friends had their last drink and made their way through the bar to the street exit. Pearl noticed Audrey and her friend were also getting ready to leave. The man looked a little unsteady on his feet she hoped the new constable, who had chosen to eat his meal in the bar with the guys, didn't notice. Audrey obviously recognized the constable because she looked over at him and gave him a huge smile as she left. She hadn't noticed the interested look the constable gave them both.

Chapter 17

Audrey was very happy things were going to plan. Almost the whole town had been at the restaurant - even the new constable. They would all have noticed her guest had obviously drunk too much. During dinner he had added another four beers to his day's intake. She just hoped the constable would not follow them out to check if Doug was driving. Once outside Audrey looked around at Pearl and her friends leaving in their respective cars. She waited until the car park was empty and asked Doug where he had parked his car. As she had expected, the car park was overflowing forcing him to park his car way down the road towards the jetty.

Audrey had parked her car in the small car park area behind the restaurant and hidden from the road and the pub opposite. She insisted on driving Doug back to the suites warning him the local cop was in the restaurant when they left and it was not worth the risk. Doug agreed and got into Audrey's Rav4.

He made a derogatory remark about the poor state of her vehicle. She explained that it doubled as her work truck, hence the scattering of sheep pellets on the floor and the piles of dirt from transporting plants on the property. Audrey asked about his day and Doug gave a blow-by-blow account of each and every fish he caught.

They were back at the suites in less than five minutes and Audrey parked her car in her Suite B parking spot. Doug staggered out of the car and went around to the driver's door to let Audrey out. He decided she looked rather fetching in her flowing blue skirt and complimented her so.

"Thank you," said Audrey. "I enjoyed your company." She paused, "Have a lovely evening" and walked towards Suite B.

"Wait!" said Doug. "Wouldn't you like a nightcap? I bought a Stoneleigh Sav from the market," he tempted. Doug didn't see the smile on Audrey's face before she turned to face him.

"Why, that would be lovely," she said. "I won't be a minute. I will come over soon." She entered her suite and closed the door behind her.

Audrey had been careful not to drink too much today and only had one glass of wine at dinner. She wanted to be clear headed tonight. She had a busy night ahead of her and she didn't want to leave anything to chance.

Audrey mentally did her checklist. She had made sure that the iron gates were closed at the entrance and the "no vacancy'" sign was hanging in full view. She had moved her trailer up to her parking spot and just had to attach it to her car when the time was ready. She checked the tires on the handcart even though she had purchased a new one recently. The tires always seemed to go flat when she carried around heavy furniture or heavy pots on them. The tires were fine.

She had her list of necessities; gloves, plastic bags, lighter fluid and lighter. She had already carried down the metal incinerator bin close to the pig site.

Audrey had been planning this for weeks, ever since the bank had given her six months to sell or pay back the loan. Both she knew she could not do. The real estate market had turned to crap. No-one wanted to purchase in Kaeo after the floods had been broadcasted all over the world destroying any chance of finding a buyer from overseas.

She had nothing to else to lose now and was determined to get even with every man who ever crossed her. Their promises, broken - over and over again. It was their turn now.

She looked at her reflection in the mirror and felt pleased. Her life had been one big stage anyway so hiding who she really was had become commonplace. She applied a stick of permanent red gloss to her lips, fixed her hairpiece in place and headed for the door making sure she left all her lights on. The suites sat high on the side of the hill overlooking the road. At night their bright lights were easily visible against the dark, wooded backdrop of the pa. Every little detail needed to be addressed.

Audrey approached the glass door entrance of Suite C and knocked. She heard music playing inside.

All the suites came with a collection of CDs and a player. She knew the guests loved this added feature. He had chosen one of her memorable CDs, "Call Me" by Al Green. It was perfect! *It must be an omen this is meant to be,* she thought as Doug opened the door to welcome her inside.

He poured her a drink and she followed him outside onto the deck where he had already prepared some cheese and breads and lit the candles on the small round table.

They took a seat. Audrey asked Doug what his plans are once he leaves tomorrow. Was he going back to Auckland or was he continuing up north?

"Thought I might wander further up North towards Cape Reinga," said Doug. "I might take in a round of golf too. No real plans."

Audrey watched as he poured himself another drink and drank it quickly. He seemed a little nervous she thought. The CD finished and Audrey offered to change the disc.

"Great," said Doug. "I am going to hop in the tub – wanna join me?" he slurred.

"Sounds great. Let me refresh your drink." Audrey reached over to pick up the bottle and accidently knocked his glass over onto the deck. "Oh dear. I'll get you a new glass – you get into the tub and I will bring it out to you." Audrey walked inside.

She went over to the player and changed the disc. "Love Scenes" by Diana Krall. "Nothing at all... I would rather have nothing at all" the soft sexy sounds wafted out into the night air. She turned up the sound so they could hear it in the hot tub and went over to small wood crafted kitchen to pour Doug a fresh drink. She had brought the bottle of wine with her.

First, she checked that Doug was in the tub and could not see her... He was, and couldn't. She walked to her purse sitting on the kitchen table, removed a small vial, poured it into a new wine glass and filled it with wine. She poured herself another glass, diluted with water, and walked outside. She handed Doug his glass and watched as he downed half of it in one gulp. She knew that the "G" had a slightly salty taste and hoped he was drunk enough not to notice. He didn't. He placed the glass on the side of the spa and asked if Audrey was getting in too.

"I will in just a minute," she said. "But first I thought we might like to lay down on the bed and listen to the music for a while."

The invitation of "bed" was just what Doug was hoping for. He lifted his large, naked, frame out of the spa with difficulty and Audrey handed him a fresh towel. He wrapped it around his waist and made it inside to the super size bed.

Audrey turned down the music and dimmed the lights. It

would take about fifteen minutes for the drug to take its full effect. She handed him the rest of his drink and he swallowed it and placed the empty glass on the side table. Doug patted the bed beside him. She looked at him. Swollen eyes, red faced, large protruding stomach, hairy chest and legs, stubby feet. She lay down on the bed beside him and waited.

Chapter 18

Constable Driver had noticed Audrey and her male friend leave the restaurant. He wondered if he was her husband. He certainly looked like he had one too many and he hoped that she was driving. He didn't want to pursue anything tonight. He was enjoying a night off for a change.

"That's the lady from the chalets," said one of the guys.

"She owns the chalets?" asked the constable.

"Yes, just up on Wainui Road towards Tauranga Bay," said the other guy. "She opened them a couple of years ago. Bloody expensive they are." And they went back to their game.

It was late. Driver had been hanging out watching sport with the guys but needed to get up early in the morning so decided it was time to head off home.

He left the bar and walked towards his car. He had parked behind the black Toyota truck. He recognized the truck as having seen it the night before heading up towards Tauranga Bay. He wondered where the driver was, most likely, at the pub. He started up his car, turned around and headed back to Kaeo.

It was another dark night. There was quite a bit of traffic considering it was a Sunday night. He supposed that the police car caused a lot of attention in such a small town. Kept the locals speed down when he was around. When he got home he saw his message light blinking. It was a message from his wife saying goodnight. She sounded tired and overwrought. He hoped their new life in Kaeo would be a fresh start for her.

Driver changed into his PJs and robe and sat in the old chair by the fireplace and picked up the book he was reading. "Deception Point" by Dan Brown. He enjoyed these last few days of alone time. He didn't get much of a chance to read when his wife and the boys were around. He felt guilty with his long working hours so when he came home to the family he liked to spend time with them. He was looking forward to kayaking with the boys. You never know Maria might even join them.

At midnight he turned out the lights and fell asleep totally unaware of what was taking place just eight miles down the road.

Chapter 19

Pearl had got up for her weekly walk to the old wooden pier and back. It was only a couple of miles but it was enough to stretch her old tired bones. Sometimes a few of the local women would join her. Nothing arranged. Just whoever was "out and about" at the time. This morning Pearl had sensed something out of place in the cool breeze and she couldn't quite put her finger on it. Everything seemed normal enough. She saw the pub lady sweeping the cigarette butts off the footpath outside the pub entrance. She stopped to say hello.

"Did you hear?" asked Marge.

"What?" replied Pearl knowing that she was right all along. Something was up.

"They found a black Toyota truck floating in the bay by the pier," she said. "Constable Driver was here this morning asking if we had seen the driver. He had checked the plates and apparently it belongs to a Doug Blackmore from Auckland. He has gone up to the Three Suites to see if Audrey knows anything. They say he has been staying there. There was no body, just the truck floating upside down."

Pearl didn't know what to do first. She wanted to go to the scene down by the pier but presumed the police would have cordoned it off from the public. Better if she calls her friends and see if they have more information. Wow. It must have been the man she saw at the restaurant with Audrey last night. He looked pretty drunk. I wonder if he drove off the bank and is at the bottom of the harbor. She pushed open her wooden gate and rushed inside to the phone. It was going to be an exciting day. Not much happened in the sleepy little place... this was something really big.

Chapter 20

Driver couldn't believe it. He was awoken at dawn to the telephone ringing. It was an emergency. A black Toyota truck had been seen floating in the Whangaroa harbor by the old pier. He was in his car with the siren blasting within minutes. When he arrived at the scene there were just a few locals standing around looking dazed. One of the locals was an expert scuba diver and had already dived into the water to see if he could find the driver.

"Nothing, nobody is down there," he told Driver when he arrived on the scene. "I don't know how long the truck has been in the water. Could have been all night," he said.

"It wasn't there at ten o'clock," said Driver. "I was parked behind it."

He ran the plates and was told the truck was registered to a Doug Blackmore with an address in St Helier's Bay in Auckland. He contacted the Auckland police and asked them to enquire at the address if they knew where Mr. Blackmore was.

In the meantime he arranged for more divers to check the bay for a body. Maybe the driver wasn't hurt in the accident and simply walked away. He may have been worried that he would be arrested for being over the drinking limit and walked home. He would check with the motels and B & B's in the area to see if they had a Doug Blackmore registered. He remembered seeing the black truck heading up towards Tauranga Bay. When the Kerikeri police crew arrived with the forensics team he excused himself and headed in the direction of the Three Suites.

Chapter 21

Audrey awoke to the sound of a siren screaming in the distance. She had hoped to sleep in this morning but that was not going to happen with all the noise. She got up and turned on the kettle for a nice cup of tea. What a perfect day, she thought as she opened up the blinds to let in the early morning sun. She took her tea outside to her patio and relaxed. It wasn't more than twenty-five minutes when she heard more sirens heading off towards Whangaroa harbor. It seemed to be quite a frenzied response to something. The noise forced her back inside. Changing into a pair of jeans and black short-sleeved top, she swept her hair in a knot and washed her face in scoops of hot water holding her hands over her cheeks and eyes and enjoying the warmth and relaxation of the familiar morning ritual. Patting her face dry on a fresh towel she looked in the bathroom mirror. Her face looked younger today. More relaxed. She looked happier than she had in months.

It was going to be a good day. She might even spend the afternoon in the garden. This morning she had planned to spray all the wasp paper nests that hung on to cactus and flax leaves before it got too hot. They were bad this year. Some of the nests were the size of melons. She would creep up on them. There were always a couple of guard wasps keeping watch on the outskirts of the leaf. If she approached too closely, they would attack. She had developed quite a reaction to their stings. Her arms would swell quickly with the poison. She always took a couple of antihistamines before carrying out the job but it still wasn't pleasant if she got stung. The Maoris had told her to put local manuka honey on the sting to stop the swelling. She must admit it did help. Audrey felt vindicated in destroying the nests. She couldn't have the wasps attacking the guests and she had been stung enough times to feel righteously relieved of any guilt associated with their death.

Just as she was collecting the bug spray and donning her gardening gloves she heard a car coming up the driveway. The automatic gates had a code written on the keypad – so guests could enter easily. She hoped it wasn't someone wanting to stay. She hadn't quite finished Suite A yet and Suite C still needed fresh flowers, wine and a welcome note.

She looked up as Constable Driver pulled into the parking spot in front of Suite C. She watched him get out of the police car. He looked really agitated.

"Good morning," she called to him. "Can I help you?"

Driver walked towards her and she offered him a seat on her patio.

"Would you like a cup of tea?" Audrey offered.

"No thanks," the constable replied as he placed his hat on the table and kept standing. Audrey placed the bug spray on the table, removed her gloves and looked at the policeman with interest.

"We have had a bit of an accident down in Whangaroa harbor," said Driver. "A black Toyota truck has been found floating in the water by the pier. It belongs to a Doug Blackmore and we are checking all the local motels to see where he might have been staying."

Audrey looked shocked "Doug Blackmore, why he has been staying in Suite C for the past couple of nights. Nice guy. Fisherman. He joined me for dinner last night at the harbor. You were there too. A bit of a drinker he was."

Driver asked, "When was the last time your saw him?"

"I offered to drive him home but he said he preferred to walk. It was a nice night and he wanted to get some fresh air. I think he had a little too much to drink," she said. "I didn't hear him come back - but I presumed he did as his suite was empty this morning and his truck was gone. Do you want to have a look at the suite?" she asked.

"Yes, that would good," Driver replied as he followed her over to the unit.

The suite looked clean. Bed made. No dishes in the kitchen. Fresh towels had been placed in the Bathroom.

"I changed the linens this morning," said Audrey.

"I like to get the laundry done early."

Driver walked out onto the deck. Fresh flowers hung in pots around the deck. A wooden round table and two chairs sat neatly in the center of the deck. The hot tub was humming. Everything looked clean and tidy.

"I have a new guest arriving this afternoon," said Audrey. "This is a popular unit with the view and the hot tub."

Driver looked at the now familiar, blonde, older woman who was smiling up at him.

"Are you sure you wouldn't like a cup of tea?" she asked again.

Driver asked her if she knew why he was staying up north.

"Fishing," said Audrey. "He said that he had come up here to do some fishing."

"Do you know what his plans were?" asked Driver.

"He said he was going to head up towards Cape Reinga and even play some golf. He had prepaid his reservation so there was no need for me to check him out this morning. I presume he left early. It is a long drive up there and back."

"Why would he be going into Whangaroa so early in the morning?" asked Driver. "It is not on the way to Cape Reinga."

"I have no idea," said Audrey. "Is he alright? Did he get out of the truck before it went in the water?"

"We don't know. We have not found a body, and no one has seen him since he was in the restaurant with you last night."

"Oh dear," said Audrey. "Please let me know if you find out anything. He seemed like a nice man."

Driver returned to his car and headed off down the driveway.

She heard him wait until the gates opened. She listened to him speed out and down the street with his siren going. Audrey returned to Suite C and opened the freezer door. The fish. She had forgotten to remove the fish. Quite a nice catch it was. She removed the plastic bag with the now frozen fillets. She was going to have quite a treat tonight.

Chapter 22

Something didn't seem right. Driver was going through the previous night's events in his mind. He had noticed the man, he now knew was Doug Blackmore, enter the bar alone. He had noticed him because he seemed as though he had been drinking. He was unsteady on his feet and his face was flushed. It is only a few miles from the suites to the restaurant but it seemed too far to walk. He had obviously taken his truck and had to park down the road because the car park was full. Audrey had arrived about ten minutes earlier. He had seen her order a wine and she had been sitting by herself at a table in the restaurant. He hadn't noticed them again until they left together.

It was only about five minutes before he left. He wondered why he had not seen Blackmore walking towards his truck. He had not seen him in the truck when he pulled away from behind it either and, if he had decided to walk back to the chalets, he would have passed him on the road.

Maybe someone else had seen him walking and offered him a ride. It didn't make sense. Why would he refuse to ride back with Audrey?

Driver returned to the scene and to his colleagues who were talking to the divers who had been searching the ocean floor. "The harbor is extremely deep in places and there is a strong current by the pier. A body could have been swept out to sea," the divers were saying.

"Found anything?" Driver asked as he scooped under the tape and joined them at the water's edge. A tow truck was in the process of pulling the Toyota out of the bay. Water was gushing out of the vehicle as it was lifted into the air. Driver noticed that there was a cover over the back of the truck and bits of cardboard and clothing were falling through the gaps back into the water.

When it was dropped onto the road Driver walked over and lifted up a corner of the cover. Inside were soggy cardboard boxes that had broken open and clothes and personal items were everywhere. Fishing gear and golf clubs were scattered on the floor. It looked as though Blackmore had his life's possessions in his truck.

Driver wondered if he was trying to get away from someone or something. Maybe he had staged his own death. So many questions without any answers.

He stepped back to let forensics get access to the truck.

Police cars, the local fire truck, tow truck and officers were everywhere. Locals were kept back from the scene by the yellow tape. Driver walked over to some of the locals and started asking questions. "Had they seen anything? Had they seen or talked to the driver, Blackmore? Did anyone see the truck go into the water?" No-one had seen or heard anything it would seem. He walked over to the jetty where some of the locals had been fishing. They said the truck was already in the water when they had arrived at sunrise. Their mates had called 111. They didn't know the truck or the driver. Never seen it before. No-one was talking.

Chapter 23

Audrey sprayed the last nest. She had counted thirty-two nests, more this year than last year. The bug man had sprayed inside and outside the units, but this just made new nesting places. Her gardens were expansive, and she knew there were, most likely, more nests hiding among the flax leaves but she needed to get on to her gardening. It was a huge task cutting all the dead fronds from the palm trees. She cut off eight to ten fronds from each tree. It took a couple of hours to load all the fronds onto her trailer and carry them in many loads down to the next driveway and dump them on her massive rubbish tip. She had to wear heavy gloves to prevent the long-spiked thorns from ripping into her hands. As she drove to the dump-site she noticed a few birds circling around the pigpen further down the valley. Audrey liked hard work and, in particular, physical work. It always made her feel good. She had told the constable she had a guest staying in Suite C tonight. She didn't. It was a lie. Tonight she had no bookings but she did have some extra cleaning up to do. She would wait until it was nearly dark to do her chores.

After an afternoon in the sun, she decided to pour herself a nice cold glass of wine and watch the sun setting over the still water of the bay. She loved her rural view. Rolling green hills in the distance and green flats in the foreground spotted with cattle. This land, as far as she could see, used to belong to one family. Over the years it had been sold off. Some of the land was sold in small parcels and homes had been built. Other parcels were larger and neighboring farmers leased the land to expand their own farms. This was her favorite time of the day. Early evening. She could feel the warmth on her face imprinted from the hot afternoon sun. Audrey always wore her huge sunglasses, she didn't like bright lights. She even watched the sunset with her glasses on.

Audrey decided to empty her own and Suite C's hot tubs and she ran hoses from the spas and released the water. They emptied pretty quickly. They took longer to fill and even longer to heat. Now they would be ready for the guests who were scheduled to arrive tomorrow afternoon. There was a family of four staying in Suite A and she had a honeymoon couple staying in Suite C. They had both booked for two nights. Then on Wednesday she had another single gentleman booked into Suite C. Audrey had never felt this good. Things were looking up.

Chapter 24

Pearl had never had such a busy day. Her phone had not stopped ringing. No-one could get down to the waterfront so she had become the town's information center as to what was going on. Her house was right on the corner and the police had cordoned off the road to the waterfront just past her house. Only the residents who lived on the road were allowed in and out. She had wandered down to the scene with her neighbors earlier in the day. Of course she couldn't get right up to the water's edge where the truck had gone in. But she could see all the police cars, fire truck and tow truck and all the goings on there. She had asked a copper if they had found the man. They said no body had been found. Her neighbors told her the police were going door to door asking everyone if they had seen the guy, Doug, anytime after he left the restaurant or in the early hours of the morning. It would seem he had simply disappeared.

She was waiting for the evening news on the telly wondering if the police had new information. She was disappointed. The news just talked about what they already knew. Except they did interview the man's wife who said they had just separated, and he was upset. She heard he had taken a trip north. She did not know what his plans were. She made it sound as though the man was depressed and maybe he had taken his own life.

Pearl had heard through the gossip grapevine the guy had stayed at Audrey's suites the night before. She was dying to ring her and find out what he was like and if she knew anything. She took a deep breath and picked up the phone. The phone rang and rang and was finally picked up by an answering phone. Obviously Audrey was not talking.

Pearl had recognized the man who Audrey was having dinner with last night as the same man on the telly. It was Doug Blackmore. Maybe Audrey was the last person to see him alive. The police always suspected that person in a murder case. She wondered if the police had questioned Audrey. She couldn't imagine Audrey had anything to do with his disappearance. Audrey was a bit of a recluse but she seemed friendly enough to all the locals. She had also been extremely welcoming to the Maori locals. Some had worked for her when she was renovating the property and others had stayed at the suites on occasion. Audrey just didn't seem like the sort who would knock off a red-faced drunk. The phone rang again. It was another neighbor with the latest news.

They had not found a body yet and were going to start searching again in the morning at first light. Pearl was too excited to concentrate on the telly. Instead she decided to walk down to see if the pub was still open with the street cordoned off. She could find out more if she was in the middle of things. She grabbed her coat and headed off down the deserted street.

The pub was buzzing. Filled with locals on their twentieth beer. They were spilling out onto the street, ciggies in hand. Most of the locals like a smoke with their beer but New Zealand was a stickler for the non-smoking cause. The government was working on having the whole country a non-smoking nation by 2015 or so. Country folk didn't think much about that. It seemed to Pearl every single resident of Whangaroa had made it down to the pub tonight. She had never seen or heard such a noisy crowd. She joined some friends at the end of the bar.

"What have you heard," she yelled over the chatter.

"The police don't know anything," shouted back Bob, a regular at the pub. "They have searched the bay and there is no sign of him. He could have been swept out to sea by now. Seems he had all his personal belongings with him. His wife had kicked him out of the house. They say he was pretty drunk when he left the restaurant and may have just driven into the bay by accident. Who knows?"

"Did you know he was staying at the Three Suites?" Pearl asked. "He was supposed to be staying there last night."

Her friends looked surprised at this new information. "Do the cops know that?" asked Bob.

"I would think so, " said Pearl. "Everyone saw her with him at the restaurant last night. She was the last person to see him alive."

The group looked puzzled. "I wonder what she has to say," Bob said. "She certainly is a strange one. Keeps to herself. Can't be good for business – losing your guests in the local pond. Hope he paid his bill before he checked out." He laughed at his own joke.

Pearl knew she had to talk to Audrey tomorrow. The suspense was killing her.

Chapter 25

Audrey had just finished filling both the spas and they were in the process of heating up to the desired temperature. She had put away the hoses and decided it was still light enough to check on the pigpen. She had guessed the pigs had already enjoyed their evening meal. She hoped she didn't have too much cleaning up to do. She knew pigs were actually very clean animals and were given a bad name when it came to personal hygiene. The local pig farmer had shown her how the pigs would never shit where they ate unlike some other animals. They would toilet in the same place every time where the farmer could hose off their excrement. Pigs liked their pens clean. The farmer brings the sows into the pens for birthing and feeding their young - then they are put out in the paddocks. Wild pigs are smart animals. It had taken Audrey many weeks to train them to come to the pen to eat.

She had left her trailer down by the dump when she had removed the last load of palm fronds. It was easier to keep it there rather than up at the main suites where it would get in the way of the guest's vehicles. She drove her Rav4 down the road and turned into the first driveway. Audrey had separated out the twelve acres into two parcels with their own entranceways. This parcel had no buildings and Audrey used it to dump rubbish. She drove down past the dump and into the valley. This area could not be seen from the road as it was completely surrounded by hills and pine trees. Audrey stopped the car when she reached the opening to the pen. She hoped she had not scared away the pigs. She let out a sign of relief. They had already been. The pen looked almost empty. The pigs had left a mess in and around the pen. Audrey went around the back of her Rav4 and removed a plastic bag of meat and threw it into the pen. She needed to keep them happy and coming back for more. She would need to come back tomorrow night and clean away any tell tale signs. Another day and the pigs should have eaten any evidence. But she couldn't leave anything to chance.

Heading towards the main road she saw the constable's car turning into entranceway of The Three Suites. She wondered why he was back again. She turned and followed him up the driveway. They both parked outside Suite C. Audrey got out of her car and waited for the constable to make conversation.

"Just have a few more questions for you," he said.

"Do you have a minute?"

"Of course," said Audrey smiling. "I have all the time in the world."

The constable looked at Suite C and asked if the new guest had checked in yet. Audrey said she had made a mistake and, in fact, the honeymoon couple was not checking in until tomorrow.

"Good," said Driver. "Mind if I have another look in there?"

"No, go ahead," said Audrey. " Let me turn on the lights for you." He followed her once again into the suite. Audrey had already replaced the flowers and there was a welcome note on the table.

Driver read the note. "That's a nice touch," he said approvingly. "My wife would like this place. You have done a nice job here."

"Thanks," said Audrey. "It has been a lot of hard work but I love it." She paused, "Are you looking for anything in particular? Maybe I can help you."

"Nope just wondering when was the last time he was in the room. Did he pack up everything in his truck before he went to dinner or did he come back and pack everything up later? It is a bit of a mystery."

"The room was empty of his stuff when I cleaned it early this morning," said Audrey." He had just left the complimentary robe on the bed, a few wet towels in the bathroom and a couple of dishes in the sink. He had drunk the complimentary wine from the fridge but nothing out of the ordinary comes to mind."

"When did he make the reservation?" asked Driver.

"Oh, just a couple of days ago," said Audrey. "He booked online and paid by credit card in advance. Do you want to see the booking? She asked.

"Not now," said Driver looking perplexed. "Are you sure you didn't hear the truck return last night and leave again early this morning?" he asked.

"I am so sorry but I sleep with earplugs in and I take a sleeping pill at night to help me sleep," said Audrey. "I have trouble sleeping and have taken sleeping pills for years. Just the PM aspirin type, she explained - not prescription. You can buy them over the counter. Last night I took a couple of PMs and I had a wine with dinner so I slept like a baby. I am so sorry. If I knew something like this was going to happen I would have been more aware of things."

Driver looked at her distress. "You weren't to know," he said "This has taken us all by surprise.

Hopefully he has just run off somewhere and is feeling embarrassed his truck ended up in the bay."

"I hope that is what happened," said Audrey. "I feel sort of responsible I didn't insist on driving him back last night. But, I am a single woman, living alone and I have to be careful of strange men especially when they have been drinking so heavily. I was quite relieved when he said he wanted to walk – I just presumed he was headed over to the pub for more beer and didn't want me to know."

Driver nodded. He seemed content Audrey couldn't offer any further leads and maybe she was right. He may have wandered over to the pub when he left Audrey and that was why Driver had not seen him when he walked out into the street. He needed to go back to the pub and ask more questions. Maybe someone did see him in the pub last night. It was a big crowd and he could easily have been forgotten.

Chapter 26

It was all over the news. "Auckland man missing in the far north presumed dead. His black Toyota truck was found early Sunday morning submerged upside down in Whangaroa harbor. Divers have not found his body. Locals say he was a guest in a nearby chalet. He had dined in the waterfront restaurant the night before and no-one had seen him since. Constable Driver said that divers will continue their search at first light today."

"We suspect it was an accident," said the local constable "and we do not expect foul play."

Constable Driver looked at the front page of the paper. What a start to his new career in Kaeo. First week on the job and he is already quoted in the national media. Today his family is arriving from Auckland. He really needed the support of his wife. They had been married thirteen years and he still loved her as much as on their wedding day. He missed his boys too.

Driver's last twenty four hours had been some of the busiest in his whole career. His Father and Grandfather were both cops so he knew what was involved in cases like this.

Although he had told the press he felt the incident was an accident there were still so many questions not answered. He looked at his notes for the umpteenth time. Something just didn't seem right. If he had driven into the bay when he left the restaurant why had he packed everything from his motel room before dinner? Had he planned his suicide earlier in the day? Or did he want it to look like he had drowned and, in reality, wanted to start a new life somewhere else? But why? His wife said they had already agreed on the separation details and she was getting the house. His boss had said he was a good employee and he had agreed to give Doug a leave of absence while he sorted himself out. Maybe he was just depressed and he really had planned it all. The woman, Audrey, seemed a nice lady and she had mentioned he had been drinking heavily before and during dinner. Driver put his notes away and headed out to the accident location. The divers should be searching again now. Maybe they have found the body. The driver's door had been ripped off during its path down the rocky cliff to the water. Blackmore had obviously been thrown out of the vehicle. But where was his body.

Driver decided to stop at the pub on the way to the site to see if, in fact, Blackmore had stopped off for a beer after dinner. He would ask Marge to see all the credit card receipts from Saturday night. Maybe Blackmore paid with a credit card. Audrey had said he had paid with his bill with a credit card. He would pull his credit card records and check all his payments leading up to the accident. He just couldn't put this case to bed. Not yet.

Chapter 27

Audrey felt wonderful. She had the best night's sleep for as long as she could remember. Today she had guests checking into both suites so she had a busy day ahead of her. On her way up to the Suite A she looked down at the road. There was very little traffic this morning. She had heard the road down to the waterfront was closed due to the accident. She imagined the restaurant and pub were still open for the local residents. It was mostly the locals on the waterfront who frequented them anyway.

Audrey loved lilies. She had them delivered to the petrol station in Kaeo every week from Kerikeri. Arranging them in the clear, tall vases made her feel like she was giving her guests that little something extra. Their sweet fragrance permeated throughout the room removing any smells left over from the guests before. The oils she used on the native timber throughout the chalets also had a fresh, clean aroma.

Audrey took pride in her suites. She tried not to think about her financial situation. She only had a few months to go to either sell the property or face forced liquidation.

She knew the locals would take pleasure in her demise. They thought her foolish with her money and she felt they were a little envious of her success. But Audrey was not going to let anything spoil her good mood. Only three days to go and she would have a new project to take her mind off things. She had done a little research on her weekend guest in Suite C and she was looking forward to his arrival.

The phone was ringing in her suite. Audrey ran downstairs to answer it. "Three Suites," she sang into the phone. "Can I help you?"

"Audrey? Is that you?"

"Yes" she answered cautiously.

"It's Pearl. Isn't it awful about the guy who was staying at your suites? What was he like? They are still searching for him in the bay. The divers have been there all morning. Do you think he tried to commit suicide?"

Audrey knew who Pearl was. She had talked to her on occasion, sometimes in the local grocery store and sometimes at the waterfront restaurant. She seemed like a bit of a busy body. Audrey knew the best way to get rid of her was to say nothing.

"Yes, it is awful," she said. "I have no idea what happened. He seemed like nice guy," She paused. "I'm so sorry, Pearl, but I have to go. I have guests arriving any minute and I still have some cleaning to do. Nice talking with you." And with that she hung up the phone.

"Bloody hell," she said out loud. She knew that would not be the last of Pearl. This was the most exciting thing to have happened to the small settlement of Whangaroa and the locals would be reveling in every moment of the intrigue.

Chapter 28

Driver ordered Blackmore's credit card records. They would be faxed to his office shortly. He had stopped by the pub and talked to the couple, Marge and Mike, who owned it. They were both serving at the bar that night. "It was one of our busiest nights," they had told him and they honestly did not remember if they served Blackmore or not. Driver had asked for the receipts from the night's takings. Marge agreed to sort them out and he could pick them up on his way back from the incident site in an hour or so.

Divers were still in the water. They had found some clothing, shoes, towels and other miscellaneous stuff. Driver had guessed it had fallen out of the back of the truck. There still was no body and the divers said there was a bit of a tow in the bay and confirmed there was a good chance the body had been washed out into the harbor and would be in the open sea by now. The Pacific Ocean was known for its white water sharks and Driver thought there might not be much of him left if that was the case.

He picked up the bar's receipts on the way back to the station. He would go through the guy's credit card records and if he couldn't find anything of consequence he would have to close the case as an accident and move on. He was getting pressure from higher up and the cops in Kerikeri were already unanimous the guy had obviously been depressed and extremely drunk and whether or not it was suicide or an accident they didn't suspect foul play. Only trouble was - he didn't have a body yet.

As soon as Driver pulled into the station he saw the huge furniture truck in the driveway. *Oh shit! I forgot about the furniture arriving.* He noticed his wife's car was not around so she had not arrived yet. Driver parked on the road and apologized to the truck driver for keeping him waiting.

"No worries," said the driver." We just got here and we're having a smoke."

Driver opened the front door of the house and let the guys in. "The boxes are all marked with the appropriate room – so just go ahead and start unloading. My wife should be here shortly."

"No problem," said the driver. "We can take it from here. You must be busy, what with the guy who drove into the drink?"

"Yes, not good," said Driver as he headed over to the police station on the other side of the driveway. "Just let me know if you need anything. I will be in the office."

It was in the fax machine, all Blackmore's credit card transactions for the past month, right up until Saturday night. Then there were no more entries. Well if he is alive and on the run somewhere, he certainly isn't using his card, thought Driver. He ran his fingers down the latest charges. Audrey was right. There was an online charge for the Three Suites for four hundred and fifty dollars. He noticed a couple of charges in Kaeo - one, at the petrol station, and another at the local grocery store. The last one was thirty-five dollars at the Whangaroa waterfront restaurant. Well, that was that then. Nothing suspicious - or out of the ordinary. He would have to close the case and tell the scuba team to pack up their things and leave the site. Nothing more they can do now.

The forensics had made their report on the truck. They confirmed the truck was in perfect working condition and was driven off the road into the bay either deliberately, as in the case of a suicide, or accidently due to excess alcohol intake. Either way it wasn't a homicide. Driver started to type out his report. Half an hour later he heard his kids shouting with glee. His family had arrived. He walked out into the bright sunny day to welcome them to their new home.

Chapter 29

Maria pulled into the driveway of their new home and parked behind the furniture truck. The boys were eager to get out of the car. It had been a long drive and they were both antsy. She saw her husband walking towards them. He looked pleased to see them. Maria's life as a policeman's wife had been difficult. Not because he was put in constant danger or even because of his long working hours, it was because she like to smoke weed and keeping her habit hidden from her husband was proving more and more difficult.

When Maria heard they were moving to the far north she was relieved. She knew it would be much easier to get a regular supply up there. Her supplier had given her a contact up on Old Hospital Road. He said it was well off the beaten track and she would never be seen coming or going. He could supply anything she needed. Maria had learned to keep her addiction under wraps. She could control it. She never got high around the kids, she just needed some weed now and then in order to cope.

Being a mother and a housewife proved more difficult than she thought it would be. It was a life of constant boredom and repetitive, domestic drudgery. She never liked cooking, cleaning, or doing laundry. Now that seemed to be all she did.

The furniture guys were still unloading the truck. It looked as though they would be there for some time. Maria joined the boys and their father in their new house. The boys were excited because they could each have their own room for the first time. Maria walked around the freshly painted and carpeted bungalow admiring the style and charm of her new home. She hoped she could be happy here. Maybe even get involved in the local community. Attend church and be involved in the boy's school. She would try harder to be a good wife and mother. She felt in her jean's pocket for the little container that held her sanity. It was almost empty. She would have to make a short trip soon.

Chapter 30

John Campbell had just turned fifty-nine. Well that is what he told anyone who asked. He was actually sixty- two but he knew he was a good looking guy and still had all his hair. He played golf almost daily to keep in shape. In fact, he could have his pick of good-looking ladies. He had been married a couple of times, but marriage wasn't really his ticket. He liked younger girls, much younger girls and although he didn't really need to pay for them, he found it a lot easier to have "his girls", as he referred to them, on tap.

Tonight was Tuesday night and he had a standard date at nine o'clock with Delia. She was eighteen, if she was lucky, and absolutely adorable with black straight hair and big red lips. She always wore red, very high-heeled shoes. John had a foot fetish and high heels were his weakness. He didn't have to worry about money, he owned his own business and times were good. When the economy was bad his business always took a turn for the better. He owned a beer distribution company and he always said: "When times are tough, women buy lipstick and guys buy beer." He was right. Business was booming.

John didn't have any children of his own but he had hired Jimmy who had worked for him for twenty years and John decided it was now time for Jimmy to take over the company. He had drawn up the papers and they had both signed on the dotted line. This was John's last week running the company. Friday he was going to take a holiday up north. He had arranged to go big game fishing in Whangaroa harbor and was looking forward to getting out of the city. John looked at the paperwork on the desk he wondered if he would miss the day-to-day running of the business. It had been a great thirty years in the beer business. He had made enough money to pay off both wives and still have a million dollar house on the North Shore. His "girls" cost him a pretty penny. They were the cream of the crop and ran him a thousand dollars a night but they were worth every penny. John liked to play rough and his money satisfied all his sexual needs. Delia was his favorite girl although lately she had seemed to be less attentive. John pushed the papers to one side of his desk and picked up the phone.

"Hey Mike, wanna take in a game of golf this afternoon? Great. I'll call and see if we can get a tee time at two thirty. Bye."

He hung up the phone and called his golf club to confirm. The pro always got him in. He rang his mate back and called out to Jimmy.

"Hey Jimmy, I am off for lunch and a round of golf with Mike. See you tomorrow morning."

Jimmy nodded and went back to stacking cases of beer. He was looking forward to having the business to himself. John was a bit of a wanker really. He didn't approve of his social life. Jimmy was married and loved his wife and always respected women. John would embarrass him when they entertained clients. It was always to a strip bar with young prostitutes. Some of their clients liked that sort of thing but Jimmy didn't. Things would change when he took over.

Chapter 31

It came down like a blanket over the valley. Torrential rain. It had been a couple of years since Audrey had seen rain like this. It seemed to come out of nowhere. She needed to check the creek in the valley by the pigpen. When it rained like this water would pour down the mountain and fill the creek to overflowing. The creek would flood and the swirling, muddy waters would gush under the road, across the cow paddocks and out into the bay. The floor of her valley was always damp due to her natural spring. The underwater spring was the only water source for the chalets. A concrete soak well and pump house pumped the water up plastic pipes to her water tanks every two hours. But when it rained, the whole area was just a wild torrent of swift flowing water.

Shit! Thought Audrey. *The guests are not going to be happy.* At least the guests had hot tubs, cable TV and hundreds of DVDs and CDs to choose from. The power would often go out in bad storms. The last time, she was without power for four days.

Audrey knew she couldn't do anything about the creek overflowing but she could make sure the spouting was clear of debris so the rainwater would run into the lower water tanks. She had two, five thousand gallon, concrete tanks below the chalets that captured all the rain water so that the guests had a good water supply. Being in the country the owners were responsible for their own sewage tanks and water tanks. There was no city service for either.

She heard a car driving up to Suite A. She grabbed an umbrella and ran up the steps to greet them. They all looked tired and travel weary, especially the kids - two little girls, as cute as buttons. She had already set out the toys in the suite and placed soft toys on their beds in preparation for their stay. Mum and Dad looked pleased to be there and even more pleased to see a welcoming bottle of wine in the fridge. The girls jumped with glee when they saw the hot tub.

"Can we get in? Pleeease Mummy?" they squealed.

"OK. Go inside and get your togs out of the suitcase," said their Mother obviously relieved the girls had found something to occupy them. Audrey left them to settle in and returned to her lower suite pleased to be out of the rain.

The honeymoon couple pulled up in their rental car to Suite C as soon as Audrey opened up a bottle of wine and poured herself a glass. She grabbed the umbrella again and welcomed them. They were very young, very happy and very excited when they saw the room and discovered the hot tub. Audrey showed them around and left them to enjoy their privacy.

The rain was not stopping. Even the spouting could not hold the deluge. The water was running in streams down the colored concrete courtyard and down the gravel driveway making long bald streaks in the gravel. She looked out over the grass flats of the farm across the road. They were almost under water already. This was not good. She checked the weather online and it looked as though it was going to last at least through the night and tomorrow morning. A lot of damage could be done in that time.

Then Audrey had a horrible thought. She was intending to go down to the pigpen tonight just to check all the bones had indeed been consumed.

She didn't want any bones lying around where the floodwaters could carry them down the fast flowing creek and out into the bay. That is, if she was lucky. They might end up on the road. There was nothing she could do but keep an eye on things. She decided to get in her Rav4 and check the storm water pipe under the road. If it needed clearing out she needed to get to it now. She put on her rain gear and tall gumboots, grabbed some tools from the shed and headed down the drive. The water was gushing down both sides of the road. The gutters were overflowing and couldn't keep up with the heavy flow coming from the hills up the road. Already the valley floor was underwater leaving her no choice, but to park the car on the gravel roundabout and head on foot through the rapidly rising water. It was impossible - there was no way she could reach the pen site. Having no choice, she headed back to her car and drove down the road to the storm water drain. The rain was torrential She headed down the bank on foot. The gushing water was almost to the top of the huge storm water drain. Tree branches, leaves and logs were trapped in the storm's fury. The water appeared to be moving through the debris, under the road and through the farm ditches towards the bay. She returned to her car and headed back to the chalets. There was nothing she could do but just hope. Hope that any evidence got washed out to sea. Maybe the pigpen was not a good idea. She would have to come up with a new plan next time.

Chapter 32

Constable Driver's phone never stopped ringing. If it wasn't the accident: it was the weather. Kaeo was built on a flood plain. The Prime Minister had even suggested moving the whole town to higher ground. Of course that didn't happen and the local residents rallied around during heavy rain to lift groceries off bottom shelves in the local grocery store and pile sandbags at the doors of the two petrol stations. Now Kaeo was about to go under water again. His house was also in the flood area and it couldn't have come at a worse time. He was lucky the truck had not left yet. He hired the truck driver and his mate to reload all the furniture back into the truck along with all the cardboard boxes of household stuff. This way they would be out of the floodwaters. He then arranged to have the family stay in Kerikeri at a nice motel. They would need to leave immediately before the floodwaters prevented traffic from getting out of town. The water was already beginning to rise. The problem was the Kaeo River. It was already beginning to spill over the riverbanks and onto the road. Soon it would be high tide and the water would have nowhere to go. What a mess. As soon as the family left for higher ground, Constable Driver got into his 4wheel drive and headed in the opposite direction towards the Kaeo River and Whangaroa.

The fire truck was making its way through the flooded streets. Driver decided to take a right onto the loop road. The road ran along the river flats and up and over Radar Point to Matairi Bay and back onto the 10, past the Kaeo Township. It was a tourist route and had only recently been tar sealed all the way. As he headed down Wainui Road he noticed that the creeks were washing the water across the road. He drove past the Chalets perched high on the hill. Water was streaming down the driveway adding to the floodwaters below. It was going to be a problem but there was nothing he could do. The residents would just have to wait it out. Large pieces of tree debris were beginning to be washed down the road with the excess water. The biggest problem was mud slips washing over the road and blocking any access. This road was known to have numerous slips and Driver guessed the road was going to be blocked at any time. He turned around and headed down to Whangaroa harbor. Mud slips were already falling down the cliffs but the road was still open. Locals were out clearing away storm debris from the road and torrential rain was continuing to fall out of the sky at a frightening pace.

Driver decided he had better get back to town where he could work on the radio with the emergency crews who were already being called out to assist with stranded vehicles and blocked side roads.

Chapter 33

Smithy couldn't find Bruiser anywhere. Damn dog. He grabbed his rain gear from the peg by the door and pulled on his gumboots. The water was already rising in his back yard. He decided to search by foot. No use taking the car it would just get stuck in the muddy driveway. He cursed himself for not adding more gravel to the drive, now it was just a muddy soup. "Bruiser, Bruiser", he called over the sound of the torrential rain. "Where are you boy?"

By the time he had got to main road he could see the water from across the street was pouring down the driveway and out onto the road causing major flooding. The creeks could not carry all the water and they were overflowing causing the water to flow over the road and down the soaked paddocks. It was going to get worse before it got better he noted. He started walking down the hill calling out to his best mate "Bruiser, Bruiser."

The local fire truck was coming up the street towards him. Smithy was well known in the area. He waved at his mates on the truck and they gave a quick squeal on the siren. Smithy knew they would be at it until the rain stopped.

Mud slips were a curse in this sort of weather. Then he spotted Bruiser. He was down in the ditch pulling something from the creek. *What was it? Looked like a bone.* "Bruiser," he yelled at him. "Come here boy!!" But Bruiser wasn't going to budge.

Smithy climbed down the slippery bank but couldn't reach the dog. The water was too deep and the mud beneath his feet was too soft, trapping his gumboots like quicksand. He yelled once more at his dog while throwing a stick at him. Bruiser yelped as the stick hit him and he let the bone go. "Come here boy," said Smithy. Bruiser ran to his master. "Stupid dog" said Smithy and he reprimanded him all the way back to the safety of the old house. Bruiser stood at the door and whined. He wanted out. "You want that bone don't you Bruiser?" said Smithy. "Well, you can't have it. Maybe tomorrow if the rain stops we can go back and find it." Bruiser whined and lay on the floor near the door. He had only one thing on his mind.

Chapter 34

Audrey's guests were all settled into their suites. They had been pleased to get to the Chalets before the waters rose. Audrey had been watching the water rise in the paddocks across the road. From high up on the mountain she had a good view of the surrounding area. She had been watching old Smithy as he wandered past the Chalets and down to the creek area. She couldn't see what he was doing down there. A minute or two later he came back with his dog. She saw the fire truck heading up the hill. She just hoped the power wouldn't go out. She saw a few power board trucks heading up the hill also. Maybe a pole was down further up the road. Not a good sign. The paddocks across the street were now completely covered in brown, muddy water. The farmer must have moved the cattle out of the flats and put them onto higher ground. Audrey liked the farmer. He was a hard worker, a quiet guy. Audrey had brought a couple of steers from him a few months ago. She liked country life and didn't even miss the big cities she had worked in overseas.

Audrey had her work cut out for her. She only had a few days before her next project. She was concerned the pigpen had been flooded and some of the pig feed may have escaped down the flooded ditches and out into the bay. Neighbors had already complained about her gray water from her washing machine releasing into the harbor and polluting the oyster fields. Audrey didn't like oysters and liked even less the eyesore of the huge oyster farms that were exposed when the tide was out ruining the pristine view of the harbor. When an oyster company went out of business they just left their mess in the harbor. The oyster beds were made of wood beams treated with cyanide. If that wasn't pollution, Audrey didn't know what was. A little washing machine water seemed a lot less harmful than cyanide. Of course, it wasn't the pollution escaping in the bay that worried Audrey but evidence from her last project. Now, that could be dire.

Audrey changed into her sweatpants and baggy shirt and lay on her bed looking up at the ceiling, deep in thought. What a pain. The pigpen had been perfect! If it weren't for the flood everything would have gone to plan. Upon reflection, Audrey decided to use the same method only she would need to move the pen up further into the pine forest. There was an old tractor road that led up the mountain. She wished she had a quad bike but her old Rav4 was pretty good on rough terrain. She just hoped the rain would stop soon and everything would have to dry up before the weekend. It usually dried up pretty quickly. Often a day or two after heavy rain all signs of flooding had completely disappeared.

Sometimes local guys would stop by the chalets and ask if they could go pig hunting up her mountain. Lately she had used the excuse that her guests would be disturbed by the gunshots. She hoped the rain would put off any shooters – at least for a week or so.

The phone rang. It was Pearl.

"Just checking all is OK with you up there," she said.

"Yes fine," Audrey said. "The guests have all checked in. I just hope we don't lose the power like last time," she added, thinking it best to be friendly.

"Better keep them inside," said Pearl. "Looks as though we are getting a lot of slips on the road. We have one down here at the harbor. The digger is on its way. They will never find that Blackmore guy now. The harbor is brown and murky. Maybe he will surface after the floods," she rambled on.

"Hope so," said Audrey wondering if Pearl suspected anything. Then she realized Pearl thrived on adversity and loved a good mystery. Once she got her teeth into something you couldn't pry her away from it. Audrey hoped this flood would give her something else to concentrate on.

"Gotta go," said Audrey. "Thanks for checking on us, at least we still have our phones."

For some reason the locals used their home phones more than their cell phones. Mobile phones in New Zealand were expensive and Audrey hated texting so she seldom used it. Usually in the floods, the phone lines went out with the power lines. If you didn't charge your mobile phone you were out of luck trying to communicate.

Audrey always made sure she had batteries for the portable boom box so she could get news from the local radio stations. She realized she should check the guests had enough candles and matches in case the power went out soon. She made her way out into the blustery wind and pouring rain to do her last minute checks.

Chapter 35

The rain finally stopped. The sun shone over the drenched farmland as the waters subsided and green grass began to surface through muddy brown waters. Residents opened their doors to a new day with rakes, shovels and hoses in hand. It was a community effort cleaning up after a flood. Chain saws buzzed in the distance as trees were removed from blocks, paths and roadways. Roadside workers went from mud slip to mud slip clearing away the damage so the roads could open again. Farmers replaced fallen fences and cleared out waterways. The town of Kaeo mopped the muddy floors and hosed down their walkways. By the afternoon everything was pretty much back to normal. Low-lying areas still had pools of muddy water but roads were clear and businesses were open to all. The furniture truck was on its way back to Kaeo having spent the night in Kerikeri along with Maria and the boys.

The police house didn't get any water damage as the water just reached the top of the foundation and didn't go into the house, thanks to the sandbags placed at all the doors.

Constable Driver hadn't got much sleep, so he decided to

take a nap while waiting for the family to arrive. It had been a tough night. He was called to a number of burglaries. It seemed as though the local lads took advantage of the flood to break into quite a few empty houses. Driver had been swamped in paperwork all morning. He needed some time out. He walked over to the old sofa in his office. It has been his refuge during long nights. As he stretched out and grabbed a cushion for his head he heard the door of the police station open. *Damn! What now*?

"Anyone here?" he heard a gruff voice calling out. "Hey Constable, you in here?" Driver got up and walked out into the lobby. He could smell Smithy before he saw him.

Smithy was not much of a bather. By the looks of him, he had slept in the same clothes for some time. Driver knew he lived alone with just his old dog for company.

"What can I do for you?" he asked.

"Bruiser found something in ditch under the road and I don't like the look of it so I decided to bring it to you." Smithy removed a large parcel wrapped in an old sack. Driver couldn't see what it was.

"What is it?" he asked as he bent over the sack.

"It's a bone - a bloody big bone. It's not a pig bone, or cow bone, or dog bone - it looks more like a human tibia bone," informed Smithy. "Don't like the look of it. Looks as though it has been chewed up by animals."

"Holy shit!" said Driver. "Where did you find it?"

"Across the road from my place down where the big water pipe goes under the road. Looks as though it got trapped in the branches and stuff. Thought I should bring it straight to you. Bruiser here found it and brought it home this morning. Last night I found him trying to pull the bone out of the ditch but the water was too swift and it was shitting down so I made him leave it there. When I saw what it was it fair scared the shit out me."

Driver looked at the bone in more detail. It was muddy with, what looked like, clawed bits of flesh hanging in mangled strips. There appeared to be bite marks on the bone. It didn't seem to have been out in the open very long, maybe a day or two. It was pretty awful to look at.

He hadn't seen too many dead bodies and thought the bloody leg bone was more gruesome than anything he had seen before.

Driver called the Kerikeri police station and asked the forensic team to meet him at the ditch near Smithy's house. They needed to do a full search in case other bones or even a body could be located. Driver thought it might be the guy, Blackmore. Maybe his body had been washed up from the harbor somehow and ended up in a storm drain under Wainui Road. He thanked old Smithy and took the parcel into his office where he found a sterile paper bag and large cardboard box and carefully placed the bone inside for the forensics team to analyze. Driver liked it when a case got solved. He didn't like missing pieces and this case had worried him. He got into his car and headed off to Wainui Road with his lights flashing.

Chapter 36

Pearl saw the police car heading off down Wainui Road. The lights were flashing and Constable Driver looked like he meant business.

I wonder what's going on? Thought Pearl. She couldn't resist it. She hopped in her little car and followed the constable down Wainui Road. She saw old Smithy and his dog at the corner by the Chalets. Smithy gave a wave as the police car came to an abrupt halt. She didn't like to appear nosey so she went around the car and took the next driveway up to the Chalets. She would stop for a cuppa with Audrey. She knew they would have a bird's eye view of the road from the Chalets. Pearl's curiosity really had the best of her. What could be going on? She hadn't seen anything.

Pearl looked for any sign of Audrey. She wasn't quite sure what suite was the office. She parked her car on the lower level behind Audrey's blue Rav4. Then she saw the "office" sign by Suite B and made her way over to the door. Audrey was at her computer deep in thought. She jumped when Pearl knocked.

"Sorry to bug you," said Pearl but I was heading off to

Tauranga Bay and I noticed Constable Driver and Smithy below your property next door. They are looking at the storm water pipe that runs under the road. Do you know what is going on? I thought I should tell you."

"What?" said Audrey, the color draining out of her face "Constable Driver? He is at the culvert?"

"Yes, said Pearl. "Looks as though they are searching for something."

Then they both heard the sirens. They were getting closer and closer and then they stopped at the small driveway at the end of Audrey's property.

There were police dogs and policemen everywhere. It looked like a crime scene. Constable Driver was stopping the traffic. Smithy was waving the locals on in the other direction. Pearl was getting more and more excited.

"I wonder what it is?" said Pearl. "Maybe they have found that guy, Blackmore. Maybe his body washed up in the flood. Come on Audrey, let's go down and find out what is happening?"

Audrey couldn't move, she felt frozen in place. "You go Pearl. I had better stay here with the guests. Call me when you find out what has happened."

"OK" said Pearl forgetting all about a cup of tea. "I'll call you." She ran to her car and took off at great speed, down the driveway and out on the road.

Audrey watched as Pearl stopped to talk to Smithy. She saw them looking up at the Chalets. *This is not good*, thought Audrey. She walked to the fridge and poured a full glass of wine. She wished she still smoked. A ciggy is just what she needed now. She drank the full glass and walked outside to the edge of the bank overlooking the road. She couldn't quite see what was going on down by the drain. She walked back to Suite B and climbed up the steps through her tropical gardens and across the freshly mowed lawn behind Suite C.

The road at the top led down to where the commotion was taking place. She didn't want to venture too close to the scene but just close enough to hear what was going on.

She followed the road for a couple of minutes then climbed down into the valley. No one could see her there. She was hidden by the hill and the valley was covered in trees and native ferns.

The flood had left the valley floor muddy and strewed with logs and branches. She walked down as far as she dared until she could see where the pigpen had been. It was now just sheets of corrugated iron torn apart by the raging waters. No-one would know it was once a pen. Audrey took a deep breath and exhaled out loud.

What a relief. The flood has destroyed any evidence. But she knew the police had found something in the culvert drain. It could have come from anywhere. She would just have to keep her wits about her. She headed back up the valley and into her car. She knew the police would be visiting her soon with more questions and she wanted to be prepared. She just had a quick trip to make and now was a good time.

Chapter 37

Constable Driver and the team from Kerikeri spent a good two hours searching the ditch where Smithy's dog had located the leg bone. It was a human leg bone. The forensics guy had already confirmed it. They took it away and would do a DNA test on it. But the general consensus was it was most likely to be Blackmore's leg. But what was it doing in the ditch on Audrey's property? It was unlikely it had been swept in from the harbor, as the water was flowing down the valley and into the harbor, not the other direction. It had to have come down from the mountains. It made no sense, none whatsoever. No other bones were found. Driver thought maybe a wild pig or dog had found the bone near the bay washed up on the shore and had carried it down to this location. But it was quite a way for an animal to drag such a heavy bone.

The team packed up and went back to the site where the car had gone into the harbor. They followed the muddy water's edge along the bank for a mile in each direction but there was no sign of any body parts. They decided to meet back at the Kaeo station where they could have a cup of coffee and a formal meeting. This was serious. A man had lost a leg and likely, his life.

Now they could have a homicide on their hands.

The group studied all the evidence and started forming an investigating team. Detective Constable Mason from Kerikeri was put in charge. Constable Driver would be the local man on the case and a couple of detectives from Auckland city would stay locally and work full time on the case. As soon as forensics confirmed Blackmore's DNA, the next step would be to confirm if it was an accident, his body ravaged by some animal when it was swept up in the storm or if, in fact, it was a homicide and there was someone out there who wanted Blackmore dead. If it was not Blackmore's DNA then they had two open cases. Constable Driver wouldn't close the Blackmore case until the DNA results came in.

They looked at the list of possible suspects who could have committed a crime such as this. The list was long; local Maori gangs in the area, known druggies and half a dozen mentally challenged homeless guys who wandered the area. Also, recently reported burglaries had Driver concerned there was a new team in town causing havoc.

Driver's first job was to check everyone on the list over the next couple of days and create a suspect list so they could start eliminating them one by one. He knew where he was going to start.

Chapter 38

Maria dropped the boys off at school. They had decided to try out the local school but she had a feeling they would soon transfer to Kerikeri. She didn't like the look of the local kids. They looked pretty rough. She wasn't particularly impressed with the teachers either. She would give it a few days, and if the boys didn't like it there, she would transfer them to one of the two Kerikeri schools. There was also a good private school in Kerikeri but Maria knew on a policeman's wage it would be out of the question. The Kerikeri school bus left right across the road from their home so it wouldn't be a problem.

Without the boys Maria was free until three o'clock. She had a full day all to herself. First she must go up Old Hospital road and follow a gravel road a couple of miles to a yellow house with a red roof. She followed the directions and found herself parked up a driveway surrounded by old derelict cars and bikes. The place looked like a dump. She walked up the path and knocked at the door.

She had disguised herself in a brown knitted hat pulled down over her ears. Her dark, long hair was hidden from sight, a pair of old overalls covered her designer jeans and Red Band gumboots replaced her sandals. If ever anyone found out she was a policeman's wife, her husband would be kicked off the force and she would be sent to jail. The cops were getting tougher and tougher on drug dealers and drug users. She was walking a fine line.

The Maori man standing in the doorway was huge. Bald head, heavily tattooed and with more gaps than teeth. His massive arms protruded from a cut off denim vest. His blue and black scarf flagged he was a Black Power gang member. He looked scary as shit. As he turned to lead her inside she saw his gang patch - a closed black fist. She had dealt with this gang before. They had a strong hold on the drug business in the far north. If he ever knew she was a cop's wife she would be dead. Thank goodness she had come recommended and with cash and was in and out in minutes.

On the way back into town she stopped down a side road leading to nowhere. Leaving the car, she sat on a log in the sun and rolled a joint. As she inhaled the sweet vapor she felt relaxed for the first time in days. Feeling great, she stripped off her disguise, slipped on her new high-healed sandals and shook out her long black shiny hair. She might even get a massage. She had seen a sign on the side of the road. It was just what she needed. It was going to be a great day.

Chapter 39

As soon as the cops left the area Audrey started with her new plan of moving the pigpen up into the mountain away from any flood areas. She stopped to pick up the trailer from the dump area. It was not easy getting the trailer out of the soggy ground and it took numerous attempts. Once on the car she stopped to pick up more sheets of corrugated iron and a few posts and drove up the gravel road to the top of the hill and through the farm gates to the edge of the pine forest.

It took her most of the day to resurrect the pigpen but by early evening she was happy with the results. The pen could not be seen from the Chalets or from the road. It was completely hidden by fresh gorse bushes and pine trees. It was also close enough to the car track so she didn't have to drag anything too far to dump it.

Once back at the Chalets she changed into clean jeans and jacket and did chemical tests of all three spas. This was also an excuse to talk to the guests and check if everything was OK. Everyone seemed happy but they were curious about the commotion by the police that morning. Audrey explained a man's car was found in the harbor a couple of days ago and they were still looking for him. They presumed it was an accident. "Poor man" Audrey said. "They say he was a heavy drinker."

Audrey was on her way back to Suite B when she heard a dog's bark. She turned to find old Smithy and his dog coming up the driveway. She met him at the top of the driveway and quickly hustled him away from the sight of the guests and onto her private patio. Smithy wasn't the type of clientele she welcomed to the Chalets. In fact he had scared away potential guests in the past. She offered him a seat at her outside table and patted his dog. Audrey liked animals. She had always preferred them to people. They were more honest.

"I saw you with the police this morning," said Audrey. "What was going on?"

"Bruiser here, found a human leg bone in the ditch just by the culver pipe," grunted Smithy. "Strangest thing. Can't figure out how it got there. Bruiser found it last night during the downpour, but I wouldn't let him stay and dig it out. He went back this morning, dug it out and brought it home. I took it straight to the police station. Gave me the creeps. They have confirmed that it is a human bone," he confided with vigor.

Audrey had stopped breathing. Her worst nightmare had come true. They had found a bone. Damn.

Damn, Damn! Was all she could think.

"That's awful. Oh my God, Maybe it's an ancient bone from a Maori burial site which has surfaced in the flood?"

"No way," said Smithy. "It was a fresh bone, still had some blood and skin on it. The cops think it might belong to the missing guy from the harbor."

Shit! Thought Audrey as she put on her best smile. "Would you like a cup of tea or coffee?" she asked.

"Tea would be good," said Smithy.

Audrey walked inside her suite to think. *What the hell?* She put on the kettle and took a bowl of water out for Smithy's dog. "Won't be a minute," she called back as she returned inside. At the kitchen bench she realized her legs were shaking. She put two cups, the teapot, milk and sugar on a tray and returned outside. "What do the police think?" asked Audrey casually.

"They think it must be that guy, Blackmore's, leg. Forensics will do a DNA test to make sure it is his, but that's what they think. Personally, I think someone murdered that son of a bitch for drug money. This town is not what it used to be. Now the druggies have taken over the town. P is everywhere. I wouldn't be surprised if it isn't those dirty low downs living in the old caravan up there by Tauranga Bay. They don't look right to me, and they are always begging a ride and money. The cops said there have been a lot of burglaries lately. I wouldn't put it past them to rob that guy Blackmore and throw him in the harbor along with his car. I saw them at the pub on Sunday night and they were pretty far gone." Audrey listened with renewed interest realizing that no-one even slightly suspected her. Of course, the police would think it was either the druggies or the gangs if there was a murder in town. She relaxed for the first time since Smithy and his dog had appeared on her driveway. She was safe.

Smithy rambled on for some time about how the town used to be a well-respected farming town. "Generations of good men have farmed this land for two centuries. We used to know our neighbors now they are murdering each other," he grumbled. "Must go." He said suddenly, as he called his dog that had disappeared to the garden and was sniffing around with enthusiasm. "Here Bruiser" he called again.

Audrey was alone again and lost in thought. Tomorrow was Wednesday and the guests were all checking out in the morning.

Cleaning both suites and getting them ready for new guests would take all day.

But she would take a ride up to the caravan by Tauranga Bay. She had seen them a couple of times walking down the road towards Whangaroa. It was a good five-mile walk.

Whangaroa was also their closest shop for supplies. Just a little ice cream and souvenir shop but it carried a few groceries and veges. She had never seen the couple with a car so presumed they had to go everywhere on foot. They could even have stopped Blackmore on his way out of town in the morning and asked for a ride. In fact, they could have killed him right there by the side of the road and driven the car into the harbor to put off the cops. Audrey smiled. She must call Pearl and pass on this new information. If she was lucky the cops would arrest the couple and her weekend plan could still go ahead. Maybe the cops needed a little help and she knew just what sort of help she could give.

Chapter 40

John Campbell awoke feeling like a new man. Tomorrow he was off on a trip he had been dreaming about for years. Jimmy would be taking over and he would be free. The feeling was exhilarating. Tonight he would call his 'Thursday girl,' Kelly, to celebrate. She was young, blonde and sexy and had the biggest knockers he had ever seen. John might even take her out for a meal, but on second thought, why waste the money? He didn't have to. She got paid enough and, after all, he only wanted a good screw and Kelly was a great screw. She would do anything he wanted and tonight he wanted it all.

He pulled down his duffle bag from the top of the wardrobe and started packing. He wouldn't have time tonight and he wanted to leave first light in the morning. He threw in clean underwear, t-shirts, jeans, sweats, his favorite fishing hat, some golf pants and a couple of golf shirts. His golf shoes were in his golf bag and were in the garage along with his fishing gear. He put everything together in the garage all ready to load into his 4runner in the morning.

He was looking forward to the fishing trip on Saturday. He

had never been game fishing before and had researched his options online. He had chosen a full day trip. Friday afternoon he would check into his suite and go for a drive around the area. Saturday was his fishing trip. Sunday he might get in a game of golf. He called the office to say he was on his way. He knew the staff was having a special farewell lunch for him and he didn't want to disappoint them by being late. He took one last look in the mirror. John Campbell was a vain man. His colleagues found him arrogant and hedonistic. Women, on the other hand, found him debonair and handsomely intriguing. That is until they got to know him. Before long his self absorption and lack of empathy for others destroyed any long term relationships, resulting in his preferred lifestyle of hookers and one night stands. Campbell ran his fingers through his thick light gray hair and smiled into the mirror to check his teeth.

"Perfection," he said aloud as he donned his sports jacket and headed out the door.

Chapter 41

Constable Driver worried that he had been neglecting his family. They had spent every minute unpacking and the boys had begged their Dad to take them fishing. Driver had explained the flood had muddied the waters everywhere and in a day or two he could take them down to the harbor and they could fish off the wharf. In the meantime they were to help their Mum with the unpacking and, if they were really good, they could play their new Xbox he had bought them as a surprise. They seemed to like this compromise and Driver didn't feel so guilty having to leave them for the day to question the locals on his 'persons of interest' list.

Driver began by visiting the Maori settlement on Wainui Road. He chatted to a few of the local Maori and asked if they had seen any troublemakers in the area. Driver already had a list of the young Maori who were causing problems and asked about them in particular.

He was told they were all at a local hungi on Sunday night. They had cooked up a few of the local farmer's weaners and although there had been a lot of binge drinking, no-one had left the area that night.

"Too drunk to go anywhere," they said. "Most of them are still sleeping it off."

Driver knew binge drinking was becoming more and more prevalent in the area. Maoris would often go on a drinking binge that would last for a few days. It was common knowledge. Driver didn't think they were responsible for the incident. News travels fast in a small town and Smithy had obviously spread the word and the Maoris knew a leg bone had been found just a mile or two from their Marae. Bones were sacred in the Maori culture and burial grounds were sacred land. Any bones found that could be Maori bones immediately placed a tapu on the land. Driver didn't think this was a Maori bone. He was pretty sure it was Blackmore's leg they found in the ditch.

Driver went to the next names on his list, Dotty and Bruce Willis. They lived in the caravan past the Marae towards Tauranga Bay. The caravan had been dumped just off the road a couple of years ago. It was really uninhabitable but the couple had simply moved in and had taken possession. They had even put a makeshift wire fence around it as if to mark off the area as theirs.

The local farmer had simply let them live there and the caravan was mostly on council land being within twenty feet of the curb line.

Driver knocked on the door of the caravan and was shocked when Dotty opened the door. She had a scarf tied around her dreadlocks and her clothes were loose, baggy and filthy. She had bare feet and stood defiantly holding the door half open.

"Yeah?" she said.

"Constable Driver," said Driver showing his badge. "I just have a few questions if I may."

"May what?" sniffed Dolly.

"May I come in?" asked Driver.

"Do you have a warrant or something?" asked Dolly. "My man is sleeping and he will shit nails if I wake him."

"Can you step outside and talk to me?" asked Driver determined not to give up.

"Shit!" said Dolly. "What about? I've done nothing." She sniffed again.

Dolly agreed to talk and walked over to an old tree stump lying on the ground by the side of the road. She sat down and reached in her pocket for her tobacco. Driver wondered how she could afford to smoke. The cost of a pack of twenty cigarettes in New Zealand was over twenty dollars. Most of the locals smoked 'roll-your-owns' but a packet of tobacco cost sixty dollars and would only last a chain smoker a few days. Dolly took out a paper, licked the side, put a pinch of tobacco in the center and rolled it like a pro. She put the cigarette in her mouth, lit it and took a long drag.

"Is it about the leg bone found down by the Three Suites?" she asked. "Everyone's talking about it."

Driver was amazed that news had travelled so quickly. "What do you know about it?" asked Driver.

"Just what I have heard," said Dolly. "You guys think it is from that guy who ditched his truck in the harbor. The body must have floated to the shore somewhere and the animals must have gotten to it," she surmised. "They say it had animal teeth marks on it."

Driver figured that Smithy had spread the word about the animal bites. Driver asked Dolly where she and Bruce had spent Sunday evening. Dolly said they had walked into Whangaroa harbor and spent the afternoon and the night at the pub until about midnight then got a ride back with a couple of the local

Maori boys, as far as the Marae, then they walked the rest of the way home. She gave Driver the name of the local boys and Driver took his leave. Dolly's story would be easy to verify, as Dolly and Bruce were well known in the area. If they had been seen at the pub from Sunday afternoon until midnight - that just left the early hours of Monday morning with no alibi.

Driver suspected Blackmore had come to his fate anytime between ten o'clock on Sunday night, when he supposedly left the restaurant, until six thirty on Monday morning when his truck was found in the harbor. Dolly and Bruce only had an alibi until midnight on Sunday night. That left six hours unaccounted for. He would call in and get a warrant to search the Caravan.

Driver still had his work cut out for him. All afternoon he went over the list and questioned suspects. By the time he returned to the station he had a list of six potential persons of interest. Two of whom were Dolly and Bruce. He would pick up the warrant tomorrow and head over there to do a thorough search of the Caravan and the surrounding area. He would need to call in some extra help. He closed the file, left it on his desk and headed over to the house to spend an evening with his family. They were having a roast lamb dinner tonight. His favorite. He needed a good home cooked meal.

Chapter 42

"Did you hear?" screamed Pearl. "It is Dolly and Bruce. They did it!" Pearl was on the phone for the umpteenth time that day. Conversations with Audrey and Smithy had convinced her. "I can't believe it!" said Pearl. "They were at the pub all afternoon and all evening. Scotty saw them getting into a car with a couple of local Maori boys from Matangarei about midnight. They must have met him on the road somewhere. Audrey said he was walking home that night and had left his car down by the waterfront. They must have murdered him and then dumped the car in the harbor." Pearl had called everyone she knew. She loved being in 'the know.'

The locals were buzzing with the news. Many were meeting at the local pub to catch up on the gossip. They had heard that Constable Driver had been down to Dolly and Bruce's caravan.

Pearl had passed on the news they were the main suspects in the crime. Finding a man's leg in a ditch was pretty gruesome. Many locals were farmers or fisherman and killing of animals was part of their everyday life. Most farmers still did home kills and were well qualified with butchering skills.

"Seeing a chewed man's bone fresh from a body would send the shivers down anyone's spine," said one of the local farmers.

"What the hell was it doing in Audrey's ditch is the question?"

"Have the cops questioned Audrey?" another asked.

The locals agreed Audrey was a different breed from them. She had lived in America and had worldly ways about her. They had watched as she had renovated that old Chalet into the fancy place it was today. She was a hard worker. They would see her working in the gardens, weed-whacking the long, overgrown grass from the paddocks and dragging stuff around in her trailer.

"She runs the place all by herself - a lot of work for a single woman," called Marge from behind the bar.

They knew Constable Driver had talked to Audrey a couple of times. No-one even thought Audrey had anything to do with the bone found in her ditch. After all, the floods could have put the bone there. The water ran down the road at a furious pace during the storm and could have come from anywhere further up the road. The Marae and Dolly and Bruce's caravan were both up the road from Audrey's place. They surmised that the bone must have lodged itself in the ditch as it was being swept down in the floodwaters.

Chapter 43

Finally both suites were cleaned and ready for the next guests. Suite A was vacant until the following weekend. Tomorrow she had the guy booked in Suite C. She had printed out his welcome note and placed it on the table next to the fresh lilies.

"Welcome John Campbell"
I hope your stay at the Chalets is a pleasant one.
If there is anything I can do to make your stay more enjoyable, please let me know.
There is a complimentary bottle of wine in the fridge for your enjoyment.
Your Host
Audrey

Audrey had estimated his time of arrival from Auckland about midday. She liked to have the music playing and the lights on for each guest's arrival. It was the little touches that count. She had changed the water in both spas and they would heat overnight. Audrey decided she would have an early night tonight.

She took a walk around the gardens. The floodwaters had done very little damage - much to her surprise. In fact the plants looked as though they appreciated the extra watering. Colors looked brighter and leaves looked greener. *Nothing like a good downpour to clear away the cobwebs*, thought Audrey. The concrete walkways and courtyards still needed water blasting to remove the muddy streaks from the water deluge. She would do that early in the morning. It was a good two-hour job and she liked the power of the water blaster and the results it left when done. It was a mindless job and it would distract her from her next project. She was pleased she had managed to direct the local interest away from the Chalets and up the road to the couple living in the old neglected caravan. She knew they were druggies and Bruce had been diagnosed with drug-induced psychosis. Hopefully she and her guest would not be disturbed. Privacy and seclusion were two of the main attributes of her chalets and she didn't want her guest to be disappointed.

She sat outside at her table on the patio and took a sip from her glass of chilled wine. It was all-quiet in the neighborhood. She could hear birds in the distance and watched a hawk swirling above green paddocks dotted with cattle. She loved it here. She didn't know what she would do when she had to leave this place. But Audrey dealt with all disasters with complete denial. Maybe she wouldn't have to leave. Maybe she could come up with a plan that would enable her to keep the chalets.

The air took a turn towards a cold chill and Audrey picked up her wine and returned to the warmth of Suite B. She turned on the telly and watched the evening news and was surprised to see Constable Driver being interviewed again. They had video of the ditch where the bone was found. Horrors! It was her place.

She hadn't even noticed the TV cameras down there. Thank goodness they had not come up to interview her. She watched the whole segment worried they would mention the Three Suites. They never did. "Thank God!" said Audrey out loud.

She was glad she had created a gated entranceway to the lot next door. No one would know the property belonged to the same owner as the Three Suites. It looked like a separate property. Only the locals knew it belonged to her.

She had plans to build a home on the land but she had run out of money and out of time. The gated entranceway had automatic gates and a keypad code. Only Audrey knew the code. Maybe this had deterred the media. Of course anyone could access the property by climbing over the fence. She presumed the cops had already done this during their search around the ditch. She was pretty sure they had.

Chapter 44

John Campbell awoke at dawn. The night before had been just what he needed. Kelly had provided all the tender loving care he could possibly want and more. She was worth every penny. What Campbell liked the most was when the hour was up Kelly left. Campbell didn't like more than an hour. If time dragged on the girls would want to talk. Campbell had nothing to say to these girls. He had slept like a baby and was ready for the journey north. He loaded the car with his golf clubs, fishing gear, duffle bag, and laptop and checked he had his cell phone and charger. Campbell liked a clean car. He had washed his 4runner the afternoon before and vacuumed the interior.

With everything neatly packed in the back, Campbell locked the house, opened the automatic garage door and left the North Shore heading toward the motorway.

He would stop for a bite to eat in Whangarei on the way. It was a halfway stop and Campbell liked the idea of a cooked breakfast by the river. He knew Whangarei had the nearest brothel to where he was staying and thought he might check out his options while he was there. Just in case he decided to stay up North for a week and he couldn't go that long without a good lay.

The motorway was pretty quiet. It wouldn't get busy until about seven thirty, by then he would be way out of the city. Auckland was an OK city. North Shore was the best place to live. Over a third of the four and half million population in New Zealand live in Auckland. As with other world trends, the rural population declines as more and more youth head to the cities for work and for social activities.

Maori call Auckland Tamaki Makaurau: "desired by many and fought over for its riches." The outskirts of Auckland were magnificent. Hauraki Gulf, Waiheke Island and the Eastern and Northern Bays were ideal for boating and kayaking. The heart of the city had everything from designer shops to jet boat trips, bungee jumping off the Auckland Harbor Bridge and base-jumping off the Sky tower. Casinos and nightlife attracted tourists and city locals alike.

John Campbell was proud of his city and proud of being a New Zealander. He knew he lived the good life and he deserved it. What he didn't know is that this would be the last time he would see his precious city. John Campbell's days were numbered.

Chapter 45

Audrey awoke with a start to the sound of knocking on her door. She grabbed her robe and went to see who was rude enough to wake her so early in the morning. It was Constable Driver. “Sorry to disturb you so early,” he said apologetically. "But we have new evidence that your guest, Blackmore, may have been killed close by. We have identified one of his leg bones in your ditch down by the culvert drain. Our forensics team will be working in the area today. We will also need to search the room Blackmore stayed in.”

“I have a guest checking in there today” Audrey protested. “It really is not convenient.”

“Don’t worry,” Driver interrupted. "We will be in and out in no time. Just want to do a quick sweep. Say around eight-thirty?”

“Well don’t make a mess,” Audrey conceded. “I have no other suite available to move him to.”

Driver promised to do his best, apologized once again and left abruptly leaving Audrey standing at the doorway frozen in thought.

“Shit!” she said out loud. “I had better get the water blaster out and do some serious cleaning. She hurried to change into her jeans and sweat shirt and pulled the heavy water blaster out of the garage. She poured in petrol and pulled the cord. It revved into life. She started first by cleaning off the furniture dolly then blasted off the debris from her trailer and then started on her car. By the time the police team arrived she was already on the upper-level cleaning off the top courtyard. The team only took about thirty minutes in the Suite and then Driver found her upstairs wiping down the outside patio furniture. "We're finished down there," he said. "Looks as though you had your work cut out for you after the flood."

"It is always the same after heavy rain," said Audrey. "The flood waters come down from the mountain and leave muddy debris everywhere. I have to have to have it spotless before the guests all check in later this morning."

The forensic team took off down the driveway. Audrey presumed they were heading down to the ditch area at the bottom of the roadway.

Driver stayed talking to Audrey. "We don't expect to find anything new around the ditch as we did a good search the other day. The flood has pretty much washed away any evidence we could expect to find," he said.

"What sort of evidence would you expect to find?"

Audrey asked.

"More bones," said Driver. "Or clothing, personal items, things like that."

"Oh," said Audrey. "How do you think the bone got there, in the ditch?"

"Could have been swept down the road in the flood waters or dragged there by some animal," said Driver. "The guys will be searching the ditches up the road but the mud slips are pretty bad." He stood to go. "If you do find anything that might relate to the case," said Driver, "let me know."

Audrey knew just what he might like to find and she knew just where he would find it. She walked inside to her suite and removed a small item from the drawer by her bed. She put it in her jeans' pocket. When the time was right she would plant it and help Constable Driver close the case.

Chapter 46

Constable Driver couldn't put his finger on it. But something wasn't right. Audrey was certainly a strange one. When they arrived at the chalets everything had been blasted clean including the decks, furniture, courtyards. Even her trailer and car looked as though she had water blasted them too. If he didn't know better, it looked as though she had made sure they would not find anything. They had used luminal to check for blood in Suite C and outside on the deck, but the area was spotless. Not a drop of blood anywhere. Obviously if Blackmore was killed it was not here at the chalets.

Driver met up with the others at the bottom of the road. They had their dogs out again. But they could not pick up any scent due to the low-lying water left over from the raging flood. Tree logs and branches were blocking the mouth of the storm water pipe. Driver had arranged for a digger to remove the debris so they could search for more trapped bones. As the digger removed bucket loads of mud and debris, the team searched each load for evidence.

The dogs began to bark. Then they saw them – caught in a tangle of branches. More bones, smaller this time. They almost looked like animal bones but there was not doubt they were indeed human. "Shit!" said Driver. "Bloody Hell! Where did these bones come from?" Was Blackmore attacked right here? One bone could be dragged by an animal, but lots of bones would indicate this is the location a murder took place. Did animals - or humans attack him? The bones looked as though they had been gnawed. Even from the naked eye they could see chew marks. Forensics had identified the leg bone as having been chewed by an animal. But what animal?

Driver knew they would be here for some time. He called his wife at home to tell her he would not be home for lunch and may even be late for dinner. They still had to search the caravan.

By afternoon the forensics team had searched the through every stick and leaf taken from the storm-water drain.

All in all, they had uncovered thirteen bone fragments all of which they believed were human and all looked as though they had been savagely chewed by animals.

Driver wondered if, in fact, Blackmore had attempted to walk back to the chalets that night, fallen into the ditch and passed out. Maybe wild pigs had attacked him or local dogs. But how did his truck end up in the Harbor? Something just didn't add up. Driver had to talk to the local farmers in the area and check on the wild pig situation.

For the next few hours Driver talked to the local farmers. They confirmed there was a lot of activity by wild pigs. They didn't think that wild pigs would attack a drunk on the side of the road as they avoid human contact and, in particular, would not be near the road but rather up on the isolated hills and farmland.

Driver then met up with the forensics team at the caravan. After an hour of searching both inside and outside the caravan the police did not find any evidence that related to Blackmore. It was a long day and Driver didn't make it back to the station until evening.

Chapter 47

Audrey was pissed. Pissed didn't even make it. She was so angry she couldn't see straight. She needed an outlet. And he was arriving anytime now. Bloody cops. They had been down on her other property most of the day. Pearl had called with the latest news. How she knew everything Audrey didn't know but Pearl had broken the news that the cops had found a lot of bones at the ditch site. Bloody pigs. The flood had scared them away otherwise there wouldn't be any bones. At least the weather was not going to get in the way this time," she muttered.

She heard a car. It was a 4runner scratching its way up the gravel driveway. Audrey waited until it parked outside Suite C and then she approached.

"Welcome," she said. "How was your drive?"

"Great," said the tall, good-looking man. "I stopped off for a bite to eat in Whangarei on the way. Great place. Love the view." He grabbed his bag and headed for the door.

Audrey followed him in and went through the usual patter of where things are and how to use the spa and the BBQ.

"I plan on eating out this evening. Thought I would check out the local pub."

"They have a great steak," said Audrey. He seemed disinterested in anything she had to say so she left him to settle in.

Damn! He is much too good looking to give me a second look. She noticed he didn't even make eye contact. Not a spark of interest. Nothing. She would wait until he returned after dinner to make her move.

An hour later Audrey watched his car heading down the driveway. It was time to put her plan into action. She took the chilled bottle of wine out of the fridge and gave it a shake. Even a trained eye couldn't see any remnants of the "G" she had added to wine earlier. Making the screw top look as though it hadn't been open was more difficult but she hoped Mr. Campbell had already had enough drinks at the pub to notice.

She carried the bottle over to suite C, opened the door with her master key and placed the bottle in the ice bucket on the table.

She had deliberately refrained from putting wine in the fridge before he arrived to ensure he saw the bottle and was tempted to have a glass before retiring for the night. Having invested in one of New Zealand's best wines, Cloudy Bay, she hoped the good looking, Mr. Campbell would be discerning enough to appreciate the best of the best.

She dimmed the lights in the suite and turned down his bed and left the room to wait.

It was after eleven when he returned. She peered through her curtains as he parked his car and entered the suite. He was too quick and she couldn't make out if he had been drinking or not. This only pissed off Audrey more. "Bloody men," she muttered. "I hate everything about them." She decided to knock at his door. She had an excuse. The fishing charter guy had called while he was out to leave him a message. She needed to make sure he drank the wine so she headed off across the courtyard.

He opened the door in his robe. "Just about to try out the hot tub," he said dismissively. He had a glass of wine in his hand. Audrey looked at the opened bottle of Cloudy Bay in the ice bucket.

She smiled. "Wonderful. Just wanted to tell you your fishing trip is confirmed at seven in the morning. They requested you get there fifteen minutes early. You are to meet them on the dock. You don't need to bring anything. They provide meals, drinks and all the fishing gear."

John Campbell looked at the chubby, bleached blonde standing in front of him. "Great. Looking forward to it." He closed the door dismissively in her face and headed off out the side doors to the deck and the tub.

Audrey had to step back quickly to avoid the door closing over her foot. What an arrogant bastard. This one deserves everything he is going to get. She walked back to Suite B and turned on her TV. She couldn't concentrate. It would only take about twenty minutes before he passed out in the spa. Hope he bloody drowns. But then thought that that would be the worse scenario. Lifting a six-foot dead weight out of a spa pool is impossible. She knew she must get him out of the spa before he passed out. She had a brilliant idea. She headed over to the deck of Suite C.

"I am so sorry," she yelled over the jets. "But you must have left your car window open and I think a possum has just climbed in. They make an awful mess."

She kept shouting. "They get into my car sometimes and I can't tell you how long it takes to get the smell out".

Campbell looked annoyed as he leapt to his feet, climbed over the spa, grabbed his robe and made haste to his car. "Shit" he muttered. "It better not have shitted in my car."

Audrey almost burst out laughing at his reaction. She had obviously hit a sore spot - his precious car. While he was outside Audrey turned on the deck lights. Mr. Campbell had opened all the doors and was hunting under the seats. Audrey hoped he didn't notice all the windows were up and securely closed. She shone her torch on the outside of the garage doors. "The possums are a real problem up here," she said pointing to the scratches up the walls of the garage. "They try to get into the garage where I keep the cattle feed. I set traps but there are just so many of them. Can you see it?" she asked.

"Must have got out," he said breathing a sigh of relief. He stepped back from the car and suddenly stumbled to the ground dropping his car keys as he fell.

"Are you OK?" asked Audrey sweetly.

"I feel pretty dizzy," said Campbell "Must have been the hot tub."

"Let me help you inside," said Audrey as she aided him to his feet. "You just need to lie down a while." Audrey held his arm and led him inside and to the perfectly made king size bed. Campbell collapsed onto the bed. Audrey waited until he was completely comatose. She smiled. It was going to be a great night.

Chapter 48

Something was still bugging Constable Driver. He couldn't put his finger on it. But something was not right. He told his wife he just needed to do a quick check around the area. He wouldn't be long. He started up the police car and backed out of the driveway. He looked at the small station on his left. It was in darkness. He looked at the house on the right glowing in light and felt a warm comfort knowing his family was safe. He liked this town. The locals were a friendly bunch. Always offering a cuppa when he called on them. Even the local thugs seemed to accept his presence. He decided to take the road down to Tauranga Bay past the ditch site and up past the caravan. He just felt this stretch of road had the answers. Maybe he could see something. It was just after eleven o'clock, the time all the crazies and drunks were out and about.

As he turned into Wainui Road and headed past the ditch site he looked up at the chalets on the hill. He noticed the lights were on in the infamous Suite C and also in Audrey's suite. The upper suite was in complete darkness. He presumed the guest had checked in.

He parked his car on the side of the road and turned off his lights. He saw a tall man stepping out onto the deck and immediately remove the lid off the hot tub. Driver wished he were sitting in a nice hot tub. Maybe he could buy a hot tub for his family for Christmas. The boys would like that. The man climbed into the spa and leaned back. He was too far away for Driver to see his features but he looked like he was fit with a body Driver wished he had. *I must find some time to work out.*

He was about to head up towards the caravan when he noticed Audrey step onto the deck. He saw the man leap out of the hot tub and follow her off the deck. *Strange*, thought Driver. He waited a while but he couldn't see what they were doing. His vision from the road prevented him from seeing what was going on. He decided to head up to the caravan and take a look. As he pulled out he spotted Dolly and Bruce walking up the dark road ahead. They were wearing head torches and carrying plastic bags filled with what Driver thought must have been groceries. He stopped and asked them if they would like a ride back to their caravan. They accepted, grateful for the ride.

"Thanks," said Bruce. "Appreciate it"

"Been down at Whangaroa?" asked Driver.

"Yep," said Bruce non-committedly. "Do you know anything more about the dead guy?" asked Bruce, making conversation. "Heard you found more bones down by Smithy's."

"Yes, opposite Smithy's in the ditch by the storm water drain," said Driver. "Guess they got washed down in the flood."

"Sounds like animals got to him" said Bruce. "Got a lot of wild pigs around here."

Driver stopped by the caravan and the two got out. "Night," he said.

"Catcha later," said Bruce.

Driver noticed Dolly had not said a word. She just sat quietly with her head down. He thought maybe Bruce was the talker in the family. They were a strange couple, hippies really. The area was full of old hippies living off the land in makeshift houses. They kept pretty much to themselves and were not any trouble. Somehow Driver could not see Dolly and Bruce cutting up a body and driving a truck into the harbor.

The road was so curved and narrow by the caravan it wasn't safe to do a u-turn so he continued up the road until he reached the Tauranga Bay turnoff. No-one was around. When he passed the caravan, he noticed Bruce was out by the road searching for something.

Driver stopped the car and called out to him. "Lost something."

"Yes, said Bruce. "Someone has taken our bloody letterbox. Pisses me off! I thought maybe you cops had knocked it over when you were doing your search here earlier today. But it is not here anywhere."

"I will check with the others tomorrow and see if they took it for any reason," said Driver apologetically. Bruce just cursed and walked inside.

Driver went back to the station and made a quick report on his evening's surveillance. Not that there was much to report. But it's all in the details he reminded himself as he made his way back home for what was left of the evening.

Chapter 49

"Fuck! Fuck! Fuck!" swore Audrey under her breath as she saw the police car driving past the chalets. *He must have gone to check them out at the caravan. He would have passed here on the way up. I bet he took a good look.* The car was driving very slowly. Audrey was pleased she had turned off all the lights in her suite and in Suite C. The chalets were in darkness. Driver would think they had all turned in for the night. She looked at her watch. It was eleven fifty-five, almost midnight. She still had a lot of work to do before morning.

Inside the garage she had Campbell tied to her furniture dolly with bungee cords. She was operating by torchlight so as not to attract any attention from the street below. Not that there was ever much traffic anyway. She backed her trailer into the garage and put down her makeshift ramp. She wheeled the comatose Campbell up the ramp on onto the trailer. She threw a blue plastic tarpaulin over him and tied the load down with heavy straps. In the silence and poorly lit moonlight she crunched down the gravel driveway. It was difficult seeing where she was going but she didn't dare turn on her headlights.

Smithy's house was directly across the road and who knows if he was asleep or up drinking at his kitchen table. As the automatic gates opened she stopped and listened for the sound of any car in the distance. It was completely silent. She turned and headed down the road to her next entranceway and continued up the steep gravel road to the top of the mountain. Carefully she drove down the mud track towards the pigpen. It was clearly visible in the moonlight hidden amongst the trees. At the pen she removed the straps and the tarpaulin and threw them on the ground.

She positioned the ramp and climbed onto the trailer and picked up the dolly. It was heavy but Audrey was built like a German tank, strong as an ox and fit as a fiddle. Her adrenalin was pumping. She felt great! She wheeled the man down the ramp and across to the pen.

The gate was open, so she wheeled him straight in. Corrugated iron sheets made the walls, and chicken netting substituted for a roof - it was rough but effective.

The pigs would smell him. She was now deathly afraid of pigs. She knew what they could do to a human body. She had witnessed it before and it was both appalling and exciting.

Audrey felt completely righteous in her actions. A lifetime of being victimized by men had taken their toll.

Her Father was a cold, bigoted man who she had not seen since she was told to leave home at fifteen years old. Later, he was a suspect in an unsolved murder of a young girl but was never convicted. Her first boyfriend dumped her at sixteen because he had got someone else pregnant. Her male bosses expected sex for advancement. Her husbands were unfaithful. Her lovers used her, cheated on her and left her when she was no longer young enough for their tastes. And now all the men wanted to do were hire young prostitutes. Women like Audrey with experience, intelligence and good conversation were no longer desired.

"Fucking Men! They are PIGS!" she shouted into the night as she released the bungee cords and watched the man fall face forward into the pen.

She had left his unconscious body in his swim togs so she didn't have to deal with looking at his private parts. Private parts she now covered with red raw meat scooped out of a big blue bucket and thrown with deliberate spite.

She wasn't sure when, or if, the drug would wear off. She had given him five times more than the usual party dose and had added anti-depressant drugs knowing, mixed with wine, the concoction would, most likely, be fatal.

Before she left the pen, she felt his pulse. It was very weak. She thought he would soon be dead. Signs of fresh rooting in the pen indicated the pigs had already been. She had left some meat for them yesterday and knew they would be back for more. Hopefully there would be nothing left by morning. She wheeled the dolly back onto the trailer, removed the ramp and threw the tarpaulins, bungee cords and straps into the trailer and drove back to the chalets where she put away everything into the garage and shut the door.

She released the trailer from the car pushing it to one side of the driveway and turned on the garden hose to give it a good wash and let it drain dry.

Audrey returned to her suite and set the alarm for four o'clock when she would drive his car down to the dock and leave it there. She had already packed all his belongings into his car. In the morning when she returned, she would clean his suite and do the laundry.

She reminded herself to give the dolly a good wash with bleach in case there was any DNA left on it. Audrey loved watching forensic TV shows and knew that traces of DNA could be found on almost anything. She should really wash off the tarpaulin as well. They would expect to find his DNA in the suite and in his car.

At four in the morning, Audrey got into the driver's seat and pulled it forward to reach the pedals with a reminder to put the seat back where she found it when she got out. She was completely covered from head to toe, wearing gloves, surgical footies and a baseball cap. There was no way she was going to leave any of her DNA in the car. That would be a disaster.

She headed off down the driveway disguised in her masculine clothes knowing she would not be recognized in the dark. She made it down to the dock without passing one car. It was an hour too early to catch the early morning fishermen. She quickly parked the car, pushed the seat back to its original position, got out and locked the door with the key and headed back towards the chalets on foot.

As she passed Pearl's place on the corner she noticed a light in her front bedroom. Pearl was a very early riser and Audrey was careful to keep to the shadows as she crept by. Once she turned into Wainui Road she knew she would be safe. If she heard a car there were many places on the side of the road she could hide. The road was lined with bushes and trees and ditches.

It took Audrey an hour to make the three-mile walk back to the chalets. It was five o'clock when she returned, and it was getting light. She had not walked up her path but taken the route up the other driveway and across the paddocks to the chalets. She didn't want to be seen entering her driveway and, if seen on the hill, anyone would just think she was checking her cattle.

Audrey spent the next two hours scrubbing and cleaning Suite C and everything she used the night before. When the laundry was in the washing machine she collapsed on her bed and passed out in a dreamless sleep.

CHAPTER 50

Pearl awoke early on Thursday morning. She looked at the clock, four twenty. It was too early to get up but she had to go to the bathroom so she may as well make a nice cup of tea and take it back to bed. Pearl's bedroom looked out onto the street. She pulled back one curtain and looked out into the darkness. In an hour it would be getting light. With her tea made she piled a couple of cushions behind her and sat up in bed thinking about her plans for the day. She had heard a car earlier going down to the harbor and wondered who would be up and about at that time of the morning. It was too early for the oyster farmers. They started around five o'clock on a Saturday, earlier during the weekdays. The first fishing boats didn't take off until seven o'clock. *Must be a local coming home after a night on the booze,* she thought.

She heard a noise outside. Sounded like footsteps on the footpath. She listened carefully. The noise stopped. She turned on the radio by the bed and tuned it to her favorite country station.

When the sun came up Pearl got dressed and went into the

kitchen. Her little dog was still asleep in his bed beside the fireplace. He didn't even look up when she walked past. "Great watchdog you are," said Audrey. "You are as deaf as a doorpost." She picked up her knitting, sat at the kitchen table and opened the local newspaper. There was a picture of the truck upside down in the harbor and Pearl hungrily read the article. It was disappointing there was no mention of the bones. She presumed the paper had gone to press before the bones were found. It didn't even mention the missing man's name. She started knitting. Knitting helped her think and think is what she did. Pearl sat at her kitchen table for most of the morning, knitting and thinking. By midday she had decided what she must do. She knew almost everyone in town. It was just a matter of elimination. Constable Driver was new to town. It would be a huge learning curve for him to know the ins and outs of the local residents' lives. Pearl, on the other hand, knew pretty much anything anyone would need to know about anyone.

She decided she would start with Smithy. He was the one who found the first bone. Then Audrey - she was the last one to see the missing man alive. Finally, she would have a word with Dolly and Bruce. She would bring them all some of her home-baked afghan biscuits.

Pearl put down her knitting and picked up a pen and paper and started making two lists. She wrote two headings: 'opportunity' and 'motive'. She figured the culprit had to have both in order to carry out the murder. And if there was one thing Pearl was sure of, it was a murder and she was going to find who did it.

Chapter 51

The captain of the Seawalker looked at his watch for the tenth time that morning. He had called the chalets but there was only an answerphone. He cursed himself for not getting the man's cell phone number. It was seven thirty and he couldn't wait any longer. The other two guys on board were getting restless. They had paid good money for the day trip and were eager to get out into the ocean and start fishing. Captain Todd called the Chalets for the last time and left the message they were sailing without him and he could rebook for another day. He added he would lose his deposit, as it was too late to replace him on the boat. *Not a good start to the day*, he thought. "We're taking off!" he shouted to the guys already downing their second beer. "Won't be long and we can catch you a fair beauty."

They left the dock and headed across the still waters of the harbor and out towards the mouth. Captain Todd liked to talk about the history of the harbor. He was proud of the area and was a third-generation resident of Whangaroa.

"Whangaroa means long or wide harbor," he began. "And, despite its enormous size, Whangaroa Harbor's narrow entrance is obscured by Stephenson's Island and was not discovered by European sailors until twenty-two years after Captain Cook's first voyage. Captain Cook had passed the opening to the harbor three times and never saw the opening even though he stayed at the Cavalli Islands close by."

As the boat headed out to sea the passengers looked at the two huge rock faces that towered over the harbor. St Paul and its twin pinnacle, St Peter, faced each other across the water. Maori legend has many stories relating to the dominant structures. "Whangaroa was called 'a singular and beautifully romantic place' by Captain Cruise whose ship HMS Dromedary sailed into the harbor in 1820, the Captain went on to inform. However, his passengers were not interested in the harbor's history they just wanted to know what fish they were likely to catch. Thirty years running charter boats, the Captain knew what they were likely to catch in the deep water: hapuka, bass and bluenose. Big game fishing during the summer months offered marlin, tuna, shark and mahi-mahi – which were what the guys were after and why they were here.

Captain Todd was puzzled by the absence of Campbell. He had asked the lady at The Three Suites to confirm the meeting time of quarter to seven. Maybe she didn't get the message. Oh well. That's life. The day was going to great. The weather was good He just hoped the fish were biting.

Chapter 52

Audrey awoke to the sun streaming in the windows. "Shit!" she cursed as she looked at the time. It was eleven thirty. She hadn't gone to sleep until almost seven am. Audrey needed her sleep and four and half hours was definitely not enough. She knew she had to go up to the pigpen and check if the pigs had been. She didn't want any bits and pieces disappearing down the hill again.

Audrey wondered why this morning she didn't feel the same elation as she did last time. The excitement and satisfaction didn't last as long this time. She felt confident Campbell wouldn't be missed for a day or so. She may even move the car late tonight. If the car were seen during the day, it would fit in with his scheduled boat trip. Even if the captain said he didn't make the trip, he might have just gone out on his own somewhere.

Audrey had to think to where she might move the car. She could ride her bike down and put it in the back of the car so she could bike back. Of course, she could just leave it there the police would eventually check it out and have it towed if the neighbors complained. The car was always the bloody problem. It was easy to get rid of the body. The car was always more difficult. Then she remembered the cliff off Radar Hill. People dumped cars and trash over the cliff. No-one would find it there. It was a few miles away, but it was all down hill on the return trip and she could ride her bike. The road was tar sealed now which would make the trip much easier. She wished she had thought of that before. Oh well.

Audrey donned her gumboots and headed up the hill towards the pigpen. It was a steep climb but she was extremely fit. Years of weed whacking the hills, cleaning the suites and gardening acres of tropical plants had made her fitter than she had been for years. She couldn't understand why she wasn't slender and thin. Instead all the exercise just made her bigger, more muscular and less feminine.

As she came closer to the pen she noticed the pigs had been rooting around the area. Pigs make a mess digging up the ground looking for roots to eat. Farmers hated the mess they made of their fields. She got close to the pen and the scene was horribly gruesome. Audrey gasped as she saw pieces of Campbell ripped apart. She turned away and decided to go back at sundown. By then the pigs should have cleaned the mess away. She headed off down the hill and when she reached the path above the chalets she saw Constable Driver standing outside her suite. She wondered if he had seen her. She stood still and waited. She watched him walk around the courtyard then he got back into his car and headed down the driveway. Audrey let out a large sigh of relief. She didn't feel like talking to anyone today. In fact she would not answer her door. She would pull the blinds and go back to bed and get a few more hours sleep.

Chapter 53

"Her car is here. Where the hell is she?" muttered Constable Driver as he wandered around the courtyard on the lower level of the Chalets. He walked over to Suite C. There was no car and the curtains were open. He looked inside. No sign of anyone staying there. He assumed the guest must have checked out.

He walked out onto the deck and looked down at the road. He looked where he had parked his car last night. He saw Smithy out walking his dog. Smithy looked up and saw Driver. They gave each other a quick wave. He watched as they past the ditch site. His dog wanted to rummage around in the ditch but Smithy called him away and they continued down the road. Driver walked over to Audrey's unit again and knocked on the door. No answer. He could see inside through the gap in the curtains. Looked as though she wasn't home. He wondered if she was upstairs and climbed the steps to the top level.

Nice deck, he thought as he walked across the large deck area to the double glass doors of Suite A. He looked through the door and saw a wood paneled kitchen with thick wood counter tops and tall wooden bar stools.

A beautiful kauri table sat in the center of the dining room. "Phew," whistled Driver. "Pretty nice inside."

There was no car parked on the upper level and it was obvious the unit was not rented. He remembered there were no lights on there last night. He admired the gardens as he walked back to the lower suite and to his car. He would just have to come back later in the day. He had some more questions for Audrey. He was also going to get a search warrant to search the whole property including the valley and the forest and wanted her to know there would be a team of police on the property tomorrow.

Driver drove down to Whangaroa to where the truck had gone into the harbor. There had been no skid marks. It would appear the truck had driven straight into the water. Who had been driving the truck? That was the question that kept on going around and around in his mind. If wild animals ravaged his body as he was walking back to the chalets, then someone else had driven his truck into the harbor, but why?

As he drove back to the pub from the jetty he noticed a black 4runner parked by the dock area. Four or five other cars were also parked in the same area. But Driver noticed the 4runner because it was so immaculate and clean which was unusual for vehicles in the rural far north. Locals never washed their cars. Dusty gravel roads created the dirt and heavy rain-washed it away for free. Driver thought the car must belong to a city guy. Most likely out on a charter for the day. Wouldn't mind taking a day trip myself one day. May even take the boys out. He continued on past the pub, past the little dairy and back towards Kaeo.

Chapter 54

Pearl parked behind Audrey's trailer. She had trouble walking up the gravel driveway in her heeled sandals, having dressed for the occasion. Purple was her favorite color as personified in her flowing purple skirt, pink and purple sequined blouse and matching purple sandals. She kept her thick black hair tied up in a twisted braid and had chosen her gold loop earrings to set off the outfit. Pearl dressed with flair and flavor.

As she approached Audrey's suite she noticed the curtains were pulled. Her car was parked in the driveway so she presumed she was at home. There were no other cars so she supposed the guests were either out for the day or had checked out. She knocked quietly on the door in case Audrey was taking a rest. There was no answer. She was disappointed. She was looking forward to a nice sit down and a chat.

She had seen the police car turn up Wainui Road earlier and wondered if Constable Driver had called at the chalets. She was curious to hear what was going on. She knocked again a little louder. She dared to walk around the unit and peek in the upstairs bedroom. The concrete driveway circled around the back of the house and up to Suite A on the upper level. As Pearl walked passed the bedroom window she noticed there was a small gap between the natural linen curtains. She could see Audrey lying in bed, obviously fast asleep. *I wonder why she is sleeping in the middle of the day*. Pearl wished she could sleep like that. Four or five hours a night was often all she could get. She realized she was holding the plate of Afghan biscuits and decided to just leave them on Audrey's outside patio table. She wrote a note "*Sorry I missed you. Enjoy. Pearl.*" It would be an excuse to call her later.

As Pearl drove down the driveway, she saw Smithy and his dog heading up his driveway on their way home. Pearl waved at them and followed them up to his house.

"Would you like a cuppa?" asked Smithy as he tied his dog up by his kennel.

"I brought you some Afghan biscuits," said Pearl getting them out of the back of her car. She followed him through the dark rooms of the ancient bungalow. It was remarkably tidy for a man who appeared to have no personal hygiene habits. He put on the kettle and she found two cups and put them on the table. Together the couple sat and sipped. Pearl didn't like silences and felt she had to fill gaps in conversations. She chatted in her happy, sing-song voice. "So, what do you think about the goings on?" she asked Smithy who was already on his third biscuit.

"Looks like foul play to me," said Smithy. "Something's going on and it's not good."

"I agree," said Pearl. "Do you think it was Dolly and Bruce?" she asked.

"Dunno," said Smithy. "All I know is the man's bones were four miles from where his car ended up in the drink. Four miles, even in a flood, can't be explained. I don't know any pig or any dog that would drag bones that far across swampy land. He must have died somewhere around here."

Pearl sat forward on her chair and stared him in the eyes. "I have been thinking. Maybe he was on a suicide mission and decided to dump his car and then walk into the bush and shoot himself. The wild pigs could have gotten to him," she said.

"Then why didn't he simply shoot himself in the car when it was going into the harbor?" said Smithy. "No. Too complicated. He was murdered. That's what I think. And the murderer dumped his car."

"I agree," said Pearl realizing Smithy must have had nothing to do with it. "And I think I know who did it."

"Who?" he asked.

"I'll let you know when I can prove it," she said as she stood to go. "I need to do some digging first."

Pearl left Smithy's and headed off to Dolly and Bruce's caravan with her last plate of Afghan biscuits. She made the best ones - decorated in rich chocolate icing with a walnut on top. She passed the Armstrong farm on the way. She saw Harry Armstrong out on his quad bike. Nice looking fellow, she thought. She knew he was recently separated from his wife of twenty-four years. She felt sorry for him.

It was a lonely life on a farm without family. She had to stop while he was moving cattle across the road to a fresh paddock. He waved at her. She waved back. "Nice weather," she called out to him.

"Hope it holds out," he called back. "The paddocks are still too wet from the flood."

As she sat waiting for the last animal to cross the road, she thought about how much she missed the farming life. Her parents were both farmers and she grew up loving the farming life. She should have stayed on the farm. "Too late now," she sighed as she drove on up the road to her next possible perpetrator of the crime.

Chapter 55

Dolly and Bruce were both sitting outside their caravan in a couple of old deck chairs surrounded by thick matted grass and gorse. They were not into gardening. Didn't own a lawnmower or tools. They were enjoying a smoke and sipping a beer in the warm sun. The ground was still a bit soggy from the rain and the caravan had leaked during the storm. They had the windows and door open trying to dry it out. All the bedding, including the old mattress, was spread over the makeshift fence to dry. Not a pretty sight but they lived pretty much in isolation and there were no neighbors to take offence. Tourists driving past on their way over Radar Hill to Matauri Bay would sometimes stop and ask directions if they were out and about. But mostly no-one bothered them or cared about them.

Bruce was still upset that someone would steal his letterbox. He had taken it from the dump a year ago. He liked it. It was a little yellow house with a door, and he had nailed it to a fence post. He had even painted a makeshift number on the front. They never got any mail, but it was a present for Dolly who felt if they had a letterbox, they had a home. Now it was gone.

They looked up and saw the tall dark-haired lady from the corner cottage down by Whangaroa Harbor pulling off the road. "Shit," he said. Looks like she is coming here" Bruce didn't encourage visitors. "Gidday" he called out to Pearl as she lifted her long skirt over the muddy walkway.

Pearl called back, "Just popped by to check if you guys are OK and brought you some biscuits."

Bruce noticed she was carrying a plate covered in plastic wrap.

"How nice," said Dolly who had been dozing happily in the sun and now felt disturbed by the intrusion. "It must be time for a cuppa tea," she said as she stood to go inside the Caravan.

Pearl was left standing there holding the plate, so decided to follow her inside. The caravan was a nightmare. It smelled damp with rotting wood and puddled floors. Water was still dripping down the walls. Dolly was not a good-looking woman. Years of hard drugs and alcohol had taken their toll on her. She was gaunt and grey. As Dolly boiled the kettle and found three reasonably clean cups from the sink and a sticky sugar bowl from a nearby shelf, she asked Pearl, "Whatcha here for? No one comes visiting around here unless they want sumphin."

"I was just down talking to Smithy about the bones they found in the ditch opposite his place. He mentioned the cops have been searching properties around the area and have been up here looking around." Pearl was feeling a little intimidated by Dolly's abrupt attitude.

"Yeah, they came around and took a look but there was nothing to find here" she said. "I bet it was that crazy bitch, Audrey. There is something not right with her. I saw her poking around here the other night."

Pearl looked at her as though she was completely nuts. "Audrey?" she said. "Why do you think it was her?"

"She has become all protective about who goes on her property. My Brucey likes to go pig hunting up on the pa behind her chalets. A couple of months ago, Audrey shooed him off and said it was private property and he had no right being there. She looked like the devil was in her. Screaming and all. Brucey said she is a crazy woman. I wouldn't wanna be a guest at her place."

Pearl couldn't believe what she was hearing. Audrey? Crazy? No way. Dolly and Bruce were the crazy ones. They walked outside to join Bruce in the sun. Dolly grabbed an old wood crate for Pearl to sit on.

"Brucey, tell Pearl about when you went pig hunting up at the fancy chalets."

"Yeah. The woman is off her rocker. We have been pig hunting up in those hills for years. She came out of nowhere waving her arms and telling us to get off her property or she would call the police. She said she didn't want the local riff raff running around her business with guns. We thought were doing her a favor getting rid of the pig, but, she wouldn't hear of it."

It wasn't until Pearl was driving back home that she wondered if there was any truth to Dolly and Bruce's insinuations. Could Audrey be a murderer? She laughed, "Of course not," she said out loud. "Audrey is such a lady. She couldn't kill a flea."

She laughed all the way home at the ludicrous thought of it. Dolly and Bruce really had it wrong. They were just trying to take the focus off themselves. Making Audrey the guilty party made them look even guiltier. Of course, Audrey would not want guys with guns around the guests. Especially guys like Bruce. He had a reputation for being skitso.

She had already crossed Smithy off her list. And it couldn't be Audrey. That just left Dolly and Bruce or someone else she hadn't even thought of. *Back to the drawing board* she thought as she pulled into her driveway.

Chapter 56

It was feeding time on the pa. News had got around. There was food in the pen. A young sow with her little ones could smell the kill from up in the surrounding hilltops. A massive boar with broken tipped tusks, mean and hungry, was in the pen ripping flesh from bones. Pulling at skin with his huge teeth while swinging his head from side to side. Others hung back in the shadows hoping they could partake of the offerings. It was a feeding frenzy. Black furry grunting pigs with bloodied mouths and feet. More pigs came down from the hills. They fought over the bones. They squealed and snorted. The noise could be heard from the Chalets below.

Audrey awoke to the sound. She had been asleep all afternoon. The early evening light was glowing through the curtains. She felt groggy and her headache was worse than when she fell asleep. She reached over to the bedside table and removed two pills from the bottle and swallowed them with water from her glass. She stretched and waited for the pigs to stop their noise. Then she would go and visit the pen and make sure it was completely clean. If not, she would dig a hole and bury any bones that were left. There would be no chance of any bones being found this time.

Once dressed in coveralls and gloves, she prepared what she would need for a clean up. She threw a spade, rake, tree saw, pickaxe and a couple of twenty-gallon containers of bleach and water. She knew she would need to break down the pen and take all the corrugated iron sheets and netting to a storage area. First, she would hose everything down. She had rigged up a hose by the top water tank and could store all the materials there. The noise had stopped and Audrey set off down the road, into her next driveway and up the hill to the pen site.

One look and Audrey knew her work was cut out for her. First, she dug a large hole. The ground was soft after the rain, and it didn't take her long to dig a deep hole. Once the bones were buried and covered with dirt, leaves, branches and rocks, she started to break down the pen and put the materials in the trailer.

Next, she poured one of the containers of water over the ground where the blood had soaked the leaves and pine needles and poured the other container over the bloodstained sheets of iron in the trailer. It would need a good hosing off, she knew. She raked the ground, where the pen had been, with leaves and needles and threw more branches over the area.

She drove down to the water tank and removed the materials one by one. Each sheet she hosed completely and stacked neatly in an area in the trees that was not visible from the path. Once all the materials were clean and stacked she went back up to the pen site to check that it looked undisturbed. She pulled a large log over the area and cut off some large gorse bushes and threw them on the ground. The thorns from gorse were vicious. No-one wanted to go near gorse. She could see no signs of blood and she was sure she had buried every bone.

Work finished, she returned the garden tools to the trailer

and headed down the hill. She knew that she would need to disinfect the trailer and put a couple of dead possums in it. She went to the three yellow possum traps she had set the previous night and pulled the string releasing their dead, plump bodies. They had blood dripping out of their rat-like mouths. She threw them in the trailer and headed back to the chalet.

After an hour of hosing off the car and the trailer and soaping them down with a solution of household bleach and detergent she was satisfied even the best blood-sniffing dog would not be able to smell blood. She threw a dead possum in the back of the trailer and took the other two up to the water tank and the pig site. If a dog smelt blood, the cops would just think it was a dead possum. Returning to her suite she removed her coveralls and canvas gloves and immediately put them in the washer machine and set the cycle to hot.

The phone rang. "Audrey? This is Constable Driver. I popped around this morning but you were not home. I am calling to say that due to the amount of bones found on your property we have obtained a warrant to search your whole property, including the valley and up the mountain behind the chalets. The forensics' team thinks the bones may have washed down from the mountain."

Audrey couldn't breathe *Fuck!* she thought. Calmly she said. "That will be fine. What time should I expect them?"

"Oh, around nine in the morning," he said

"Good, I will expect them then," said Audrey.

"Goodnight Constable Driver." She hung up the phone and collapsed on the bed.

Chapter 57

He could hear them. Squealing and snorting! They obviously caught some animal. He had to keep Bruiser inside. The wild pigs were making him go crazy. Smithy would take him pig hunting often. The sound of the pigs could be heard across the valley. He was tempted to go over the road and see what the commotion was. But he always felt a little unwelcome at Audrey's. He could tell she didn't like the way he dressed or the fact his beard had been left untouched for as long as he could remember. Bathing was not his favorite activity. And he didn't feel it was necessary to wash his clothes every day, as they just got dirty again.

He turned up the TV a little louder to listen to the six o'clock news. When the news was over he decided to take Bruiser for a walk. The pigs had stopped squealing and it was a lovely evening. As he walked out onto the road, he looked up at the pa. He noticed Audrey's car coming down the hill. Looked as though she had been checking the possum traps. *Not a job for a lady*, thought Smithy pulling dead possums out of traps. He headed down the road towards Whangaroa. Bruiser was pleased to be out with his master. The couple walked at a fast pace. Smithy was fit for an old guy. He didn't want anyone to know he would be turning seventy-three on his next birthday. Not that he celebrated birthdays.

He thought about Pearl's visit earlier in the day. She seemed to be pretty fixated on the dead guy. He guessed she didn't have much excitement in her life and a murder gave her a reason for living. *Was she right about Dolly and Bruce?* he wondered. Somehow he couldn't see the drugged out couple doing anything so energetic, let alone diabolical in nature. They seemed pretty harmless. He had seen them many times down at the local pub. They kept pretty much to themselves. He often saw them walking home from Whangaroa. They didn't work. He figured they lived on a benefit.

On the way back up the hill Bruiser suddenly started to go crazy. He started digging in the ground and barking his head off. "What the bloody hell!" Smithy yelled. "Get outta there!" He threw a small stone at him and Bruiser reluctantly came back to his side. "Whatcha think ya doing?" growled Smithy. "Have you gone bone mad?" They made it home without another incident. Smithy decided he felt like lamb chops, mashed potatoes and gravy for his tucker. He was a good cook. Meat and potatoes - that was his specialty. The man and his dog looked forward to a good feed.

Chapter 58

Audrey had been pacing up and down for over an hour. She knew she could not possibly have got rid of all the human blood up the hill. She had only one alternative; she had to kill one of her lambs and dump the body up there. Once the pigs attacked the animal and spread its blood around, there would be enough of a mess that the cops wouldn't even suspect the sheep's blood was mixed with human blood. There was only one problem. Audrey loved animals as much as she hated men. She would have to sacrifice a lamb and it would break her heart. "Fucking Men!" she spat. "They are the cause of everything that has gone wrong in my life. Even dead, they cause problems". She knew she couldn't let the pigs eat her lamb alive. She would have to kill it first and then dump it at the site. The pigs would smell the kill and come down to feed.

Pigs would eat whenever there was food to eat. She had learned that from the pig farmer next door. He would feed the baby pigs copious amounts of milk in a trough twice a day along with pig meal. They would eat and eat and eat. Over-feeding meant bigger weaners. Now she was going to feed one of her pet lambs to the pigs. She knew she had no choice. *That bloody Constable Driver just won't let things lie. Now he has to go sniffing around my place. He needs something else to take his mind of Blackmore.*

Something else was worrying Audrey. She needed to move Campbell's car from the waterfront and dump it over Radar Hill. It had been parked there all day and it would start to cause attention if it was left there overnight. But she would have to deal with the lamb first. She went outside to the garage and filled a bucket with multigrain nuts and headed for the sheep paddock. The farmer next door, Harry Armstrong, had been kind enough to loan her three sheep to help keep the grass down on the lower paddocks. Originally they were wild sheep but Audrey had tamed them with pellets and a regular feeding schedule.

One of the sheep, Snow White, had a baby lamb. It had a black and white face like her Mother. Audrey loved her sheep. One of her favorite times of the day was when she would walk into the sheep paddock and call them to her. They would come running towards her and eat out of her bucket.

Tonight she knew feeding time would never be the same again. She would do it quickly and as painlessly as possible and then drive the little lamb up to the pen site and dump her body there. By the time Audrey had laid her pet to rest among the leaves and branches of the forest she had cried her tears dry. She sat down on the forest floor and decided even punishing the crudest men for their crimes was not worth having to kill a little lamb.

Audrey returned to the chalets and dressed in black jeans, black sweatshirt and donned her black baseball hat. She wheeled her bike out of the garage and started down the driveway and out onto the street.

It was getting dark. She turned on her bike lights and tucked her blonde hair into her cap. She knew no-one would recognize her. It only took thirty minutes to bike to his car parked by the dock. She made sure no one was around, and quickly opened up the back of the 4runner and put her bike inside. She opened the driver's door, pushed the seat forward and drove out of the harbor and back up Wainui Road to Radar Hill.

She was pleased that living in a small town with an almost nonexistent population made it easy to come and go in the shadows without being noticed. Twenty minutes later she was at the top of Radar Hill and looking down at the dump area seventy feet below. She had not passed any cars on the road and knew at this time of night it would be unlikely to see any traffic. She hoped the sound of the car veering down the bank would not be heard by distant neighbors and decided it would be quieter to push the car over the cliff without the engine running. She remembered to put the seat back to where it was, and with the keys turned on in the ignition, the wheel turned towards the cliff and the car in neutral, she walked around the back of the car and removed her bike. As she pushed the car over the cliff she was amazed how easily it rolled down the hill and landed in the bush below. It was completely hidden by the gorse and bush down the cliff. It had made very little noise, much less than she thought it would. The job was done. It was over.

Audrey felt elated as she biked down the hill, past the caravan, past the Maori Marae, past Harry Armstrong's farm and back home. She felt so good after her ride, she poured herself an extra big glass of wine and settled in for an early evening. She would need her wits for the cop search tomorrow at nine. She hoped the dead possums and her sweet dead lamb were doing their job of disguising her wicked deeds. Little did the cops know there were two missing men consumed by local wild pigs. If it weren't for the little lamb, today would have been another perfect day.

At eleven o'clock, as Audrey reached over and turned out her bedside light, she heard the pigs squealing and scrapping up on the pa. Her heart sank. They were eating her little baby lamb. "Fucking men," she said as she rolled over to go to sleep.

Chapter 59

Constable Driver had a late start. There were a couple of burglaries down in Kaeo last night and he had not got to bed until the early hours of the morning. With warrant in hand he headed off to the search site at Audrey's. When he pulled into the driveway he noticed the team had already arrived. Audrey had opened the gates and was talking to the officers. "Thanks Audrey," said Driver. "Sorry I am a little late. Here is the search warrant." He handed her the paperwork.

Audrey gave it a quick look. "I'll head up to the chalets. If you need me, you know where to find me." Audrey noticed they had brought the dogs. She wondered if they would be searching inside the suites. Of course they would. When she reached Suite B the phone was ringing. It was Pearl.

"I saw all the cops heading your way," panted Pearl. "Are they at your place?"

"Yes. I can't talk now I have to run out and get some supplies. I'll catch you later." Audrey hung up the phone. Pearl was not what she needed right now. She needed to think.

She grabbed her purse and headed off to her car. She would

drive down to Kaeo and pick up some supplies. As she turned into her other driveway, Audrey opened her window and called out to Constable Driver. "I am off to the shop. I'll be back soon. You are all welcome to come up for morning tea at half past ten," she said.

"Great," said Driver "That is kind of you. I will tell the boys."

The trip into Kaeo was uneventful. The locals were curious about the bones found on her property. Audrey said she was shocked about the findings and would be pleased when the police finished their investigation. She was worried what it would do for business having the police around. She stopped for petrol at the fuel stop and again, the conversation focused on the bones. No-one wanted to call it a murder and yet an accident seemed less likely. Audrey was pleased when she arrived back at the chalets. No-one even slightly suspected her.

The group arrived at exactly ten-thirty. Audrey had set up a nice spread upstairs on the large deck of Suite A. There was seating for twelve and every seat was taken. She had picked up the moist carrot cake from the Kaeo bakery and offered savory biscuits with cheese and tomato. She poured out the tea and coffee and said for the men to help themselves. Some of the guys lit up cigarettes. They had put the dogs back in the cars. Audrey asked if the dogs needed any water. They said they had already been taken care of. She listened as they talked. They had searched the lower swampy paddocks and after morning tea they were going to search up on the pa. They had found nothing of any interest so far. The flood had washed away any scent or evidence of Blackmore being in the area. Audrey knew the worse was yet to come. She excused herself and went inside to the kitchen. She knew her nice, relaxed demeanor would prevent any suspicions they may have about her. Audrey was a pro at hiding her feelings.

Suddenly she could hear cell phones going off. She went

outside to see what was causing the commotion. The police were suddenly very animated.

"Sorry Audrey, we have to go. We will be back when we can," said Driver as he picked up his hat and headed off down the steps to where his car was parked.

Within minutes the deck was empty and cars were speeding down her driveway with their lights flashing. There was obviously an emergency. Audrey racked her brains trying to figure out what could possibly have happened. Did she miss something? She noticed the cars had gone up towards Tauranga Bay. She could hear their sirens now fading in the distance. Are they going up Radar Hill? Surely they haven't found the car.

What should she do? Should she follow them? No, why would she do that? It would only draw attention to her. She must be patient, wait and see. In the meantime she would go to the pen site. She could now work on getting rid of any human blood that may have been left there. She changed into her jeans, put on her gumboots and headed on up the hill.

Audrey had done research online to find out how to get rid of the blood off the ground with no result. Even disinfectants cannot totally get rid of blood. It can still be seen with luminal. She had remembered last night she had a dozen bags of blood and bone fertilizer in her garage. She had a plan. She piled her gardening tools into her trailer along with bags of topsoil and fertilizer and headed up to the site.

By the afternoon she had cleared a good size patch of ground and spread the topsoil, blood and bone and sheep fertilizer, She used the corrugated iron panels and posts to create a wall around the freshly formed garden area. When Audrey had driven into Kaeo she had picked up a selection of vegetable plants. Now she plantedthem neatly in rows. Placing the chicken netting over the whole area to keep out the birds and animals was the final step.

She stood back and looked at the results of her labor. Much better, she thought. She had tossed her poor little lamb's remains further up in the forest. The police dogs may smell the dead animal. She had read it was difficult for dogs to differentiate between animal and human blood. She pulled the hose to the garden area and gave everything a final watering. She was proud of the result. She wondered if the police would even bother to come back again. Audrey felt a lot more confident that she had outsmarted them all. *I need a nice glass of wine to celebrate,* she thought as she collected all her tools and the empty bags and put them in the trailer and headed off down the hill towards the chalets.

Chapter 60

Sure enough, it was the same 4runner Driver had seen parked at Whangaroa on Saturday. He also remembered seeing the car leave the restaurant in Whangaroa the night before and head up Wainui Road. He was sure of it. He had noticed it because it had looked so clean and out of place. Some young local boys had climbed down the cliff face to search for stuff they could sell they told the police. "People just dump stuff over the cliff" one of the young Maori boys told him. "Good stuff too. We tie a rope around it and pull it up. When we saw the flash, new 4runner we thought we should call the cops incase people are lying around here dead or hurt or something. It wasn't here yesterday so it must have fallen down here last night."

The police and the dogs searched the area at the base of the cliff. There was no sign of anyone. The car had golf clubs, fishing gear and a suitcase inside filled with a man's clothing and personal items. The police called the local towing service and while they waited they checked for any identification that might have been left inside. There was no wallet or ID in the car. They were careful not to disturb anything.

Driver called in the plate number and they quickly responded with the name: John Campbell, address: 872 Longs Drive, Devonport, Auckland. "Wonder what he was doing up here?" he said. "And if anyone else was traveling with him? I saw this car yesterday parked down by the dock. Maybe he had booked a fishing trip. He must be around here somewhere. Search again," he said. "Looks as though we may have another missing guy. What's going on around here?"

By the time the tow truck had taken the 4runner away. The police had spent a couple of hours searching for the body.

"Maybe he survived the fall and simply climbed up the cliff and hitched a ride somewhere," said one of the detectives. "He definitely is not here or the dogs would have found him by now. It is unlikely he wandered off down here in the valley unless he was badly hurt."

"Let's leave a couple of guys and the dogs here while we check out the area to see if anyone saw anything. I will call around the fishing charters to see if he booked a trip," said Driver.

The team split into three. It was going to be another long day. As Constable Driver drove back towards Whangaroa Harbor he wondered, did they have a murderer on the loose, or was it simply a coincidence that two cars were being driven over banks and their occupants were not found at the scene? Did this John Campbell and Doug Blackmore have anything in common? Was there any connection? What did he know about them? He started a mental list. Both men came from Auckland. Both men were fishermen based on the fishing gear in the cars. Both men were golfers. Both men were in their late fifties, early sixties. Both men's cars were found abandoned and wrecked but all their personal items remained in the cars so it can't have been a robbery.

He needed to get back to his office and make a detailed list. But first he would check out the local game fishing office to enquire if John Campbell had hired a charter boat.

After Constable Driver had spoken with Captain Todd and learned that, indeed a John Campbell had booked a day trip on his boat, and had not turned up for the seven o'clock departure, he knew that something wasn't right. Driver had seen Campbell's car parked at the dock. Why didn't he board the boat? How did his car end up over Radar Hill? He had asked the Captain if he had a local phone number for Campbell. He said the Three Suites at Whangaroa were his contact and had left a number of messages with the lady there. Constable Driver was shocked. Two more things the men had in common. He guessed the man he had seen getting into the hot tub in Suite C was, in fact, the now missing, John Campbell. He also remembered seeing him get out the hot tub in haste and follow Audrey somewhere. *But where?* he wondered. Time to get back to the office and make some calls. First he would call Campbell's family. He would need to track them down first.

Chapter 61

She heard a quad bike coming up the driveway. She was pleasantly surprised to see it was her neighbor, Harry Armstrong. She walked out to meet him on the driveway. He was a good-looking man. Tall, lean, rugged body, topped with a cowboy hat. He sat astride the bike, wearing gumboots and smoking his cigarette. His loyal old cattle dog sat behind him. He always seemed so shy. Audrey liked his demeanor. He was not loud and arrogant like the other men in her life. She thought he was married and she knew he had children. She had met his wife a year or so ago. She was a pretty blonde woman.

"Just checking on the sheep," he said. "We will need to get them sheared in December."

Audrey invited him in for a coffee and was surprised when the shy man accepted. He tied his dog with an old string to his bike and followed her to the outside table on her patio. Audrey went inside to make the coffee. Harry sat outside smoking his cigarette.

"How are your wife and family?" Audrey called out.

"My wife and I are separated," he replied. "She has got herself tied up with a drunk. I'm worried about the kids," he said.

"I am so sorry, said Audrey. "Divorce is an awful thing. I know. But it gets easier in time."

"Yeah the divorce is costing me big time," he said, looking sad and angry.

Over coffee the two shared stories about going through the divorce process. Audrey liked his company. He was easy to talk to. She explained the little lamb had gone missing and she had found it on the pa this afternoon when she was making a vegetable garden up there. "Looked as though the wild pigs got to it," she said. It must have escaped under the fence."

"Do you want me take it away?" asked Harry.

"Would you? asked Audrey looking helpless. "That would be great. It is so sad losing her. She was my favorite."

Audrey climbed on the back of his quad bike with the dog and off they went down the road and up the driveway next door to the new garden site. She could feel the warmth of his body as she wrapped her arms around his waist for support.

Harry was impressed with her new vegetable garden. She had cleared the bush away from the site to allow the sun to get to the garden. Yet it was sheltered enough to prevent wind damage. "Good job," he said obviously impressed. "The veges should do well here. Where is the lamb?"

Audrey led him further up the hill to where she had thrown the lamb's remains.

"Yeah, wild pigs, alright. I had better come up here later with my rifle and the dogs. You don't want wild pigs wandering around your property."

Audrey nodded and said she was grateful for his help.

He put what was left of the little lamb in an old food sack he had tied to the bike and threw it on the front rack of his bike. His dog had already leapt off the bike and was sniffing around with interest. "He can smell the pigs," said Harry. "Looks as though there are at least four or five of them" he commented studying the ground.

On the way back down Harry checked out the other sheep. He was impressed how Audrey had tamed them. She was obviously fond of animals. Anyone who loved animals had to be a good person, he thought. He dropped Audrey at the chalets and headed back to his farm. After dinner he would get the other dogs and head back up to the pa. Audrey had installed a gate between their properties so that the cattle could cross through. He would take that route so as not to disturb her.

Plus it would take more than one trip if he shot more than one pig. He liked pig hunting. It was his favorite sport. Many an evening he would go up to the hills behind his farm with his dogs and bring back a pig. Sometimes he would capture wild weaners and bring them back to the pigpen, fatten them up and sell them to the local Maoris. Wild pigs fed on cows' milk were popular with the locals. In fact, pigs were Harry's favorite animals. His father had liked pigs and so did he. He had eighty pigs at the moment. It was a busy time. By Christmas they would all be gone. Except, of course for his sows. He had nine sows and two boars, the rest were all being fattened for sale. He knew Audrey did not like pigs. He had told her once about how vicious they can be and now she was terrified of them. He hadn't meant to scare her. Audrey's biggest love was her cattle. He had sold her two steers a year ago and she had tamed them too.

He was looking forward to going pig hunting tonight. It was best just after dark.

Chapter 62

Audrey hadn't even heard the gunshots. She had gone to sleep early and slept all night. Just before she woke she had a wonderful dream. It seemed so real that she awoke embarrassed and feeling very vulnerable. She had dreamed about her neighbor, Harry Armstrong. They were making love and she had never felt so wonderful in all her life. He had been so loving and caring towards her. No man had ever treated her that way before. It took a few minutes after she had awoken from the dream to realize it hadn't happened. It was only a dream. She lay quietly in bed for some time reveling in the blissful feeling of being in love.

Audrey had stopped dating over a year ago. That was when the darkness came. She had joined a couple of Internet dating sites when she had returned to New Zealand eight years ago. She would choose a couple of men from the hundred or so who had responded.

After talking with them by phone she would invite them to the chalets for a romantic evening of dancing, wine and music. The date came complete with overnight accommodation as most of her dates drove from Auckland or further afield. It was always made clear she did not sleep with anyone on a first date. She was looking for a long-term relationship and wanted to get to know someone first. After all, legalized prostitution gave men, who just wanted sex, an alternative to dating.

It wasn't long before she realized she had confused New Zealand men with American men who actually knew what a date was; a nice dinner, good conversation, a time to get to know each other and to find out if there is enough chemistry, or interest, to pursue the relationship further. She had dated in America for many years but was not really attracted to American men. Seven years of dating, entertaining, wining and dining in New Zealand turned out to be a nightmare from hell. New Zealand men, she had found to be arrogant, egotistical, self- opinionated, crude, chauvinistic and, more importantly, sexually aggressive and romantically ignorant.

Once she had invited a city lawyer to dinner. She had prepared his suite with his favorite wine and favorite CDs. She planned a crayfish dinner (caught fresh the same day) with a Waldorf salad and homemade apple sponge pudding for desert. She had shopped all day, dressed in her most feminine outfit and filled the spa with clean scented water. The "no vacancy" sign was displayed prominently for the whole weekend.

When her lawyer arrived he was wearing a linen shirt, baggy linen pants and bare feet. After a quick hello he immediately ran frantically to the top of the pa behind the chalets. Shocked, Audrey changed shoes and followed him up the steep incline with equal stamina. By the time they returned to the deck of Suite A to her prepared champagne and snacks, she was sweating profusely and extremely confused. The man was obviously on something.

For the first hour they watched the sun set, drank champagne, danced and talked. It was nice. Audrey prepared the meal in the downstairs kitchen while her date went upstairs to the lounge and dining room overlooking the harbor.

The table was set for two. Audrey carried the carefully prepared meals up the stairs. As she entered the room her date stood to reveal he had removed his trousers and underwear and was clad only in his open, gaping shirt - his willy protruding rudely in stiff acknowledgement of her presence. She felt completely disgusted and horribly disappointed. Not knowing how to respond, she simply walked to the table, placed the meals on her beautifully hand woven tablemats and took her seat. He nonchalantly walked over to join her.

The evening went from bad to worse. He wouldn't go to his own suite but instead insisted on sleeping in her bed "I won't touch you. I just want to lie beside you," he repeated so many times Audrey just gave in. All she wanted to do was to go sleep and forget the whole event.

The next morning he departed after she had cooked a wonderful bacon and egg breakfast. He texted her in the afternoon upon his return home; *"I had wonderful time. Hope we can do it again sometime."*

Always the hostess, Audrey would entertain date after date. Most men removed their clothes within the first hour. All men wanted to have sex as soon as possible. Once or twice she did sleep with a man to whom she was attracted but he would mistakenly think having sex meant they were now a couple and he wouldn't want to leave.

Audrey had been both mentally and visually abused by men for as long as she could remember. She couldn't remember the last time she even liked the look of a penis. She thought that in her sexual past, the sight of a penis might have stirred a positive reaction but years of men presenting their prize organ to her as though they were offering her a gift she just couldn't refuse had destroyed any positive sexual feeling ever associated with them.

When Audrey was a young woman in her early thirties she remembered a meeting, which had been arranged with a businessman from out of town. She was excited to be presenting her idea to a possible investor. The meeting was held in his hotel suite. As she sat down at the glass coffee table and removed her presentation from her briefcase, he immediately removed his very large, naked, extended penis and presented it proudly six inches from her face.

During her many careers, she had became more and more horrified by men's appalling sexual behavior. Bosses attempting to rape her in her teen years to grown men in their fifties acting like animals in the presence of a lady.

She had even accepted a meeting on a Boeing 747 from LAX to Heathrow with a businessman who said it was the only time he had available to discuss investing in her new company. Once aboard, he postponed the meeting until they were at their hotel. Audrey, dressed in her most appropriate business attire complete with loan documents and high hopes, was greeted at the door by the gentleman in his bathrobe. She apologized for interrupting him and suggested she return back when he was dressed and ready for the meeting. That was not to happen. That was never to happen. The next few hours of his physical naked advances finally ended with him wanking off beside her on the bed. Sad and disgusted Audrey fled to her sister's house in London. She took the next plane back home.

A seething anger had been growing inside Audrey's mind since she was a small child. It had now matured into an uncompromising hatred towards men. Hence she was surprised by the fondness she was feeling towards Harry Armstrong. She hoped he had killed the pigs. He could collaborate her problem she was having with wild pigs if ever the police pursued her further. She wondered if he would come by again today. She hoped so.

Chapter 63

It was more difficult than he thought. There were a number of John Campbell's living in Auckland and the address on his registration was not current. He did a search, but without his driver's license or current address it was proving difficult. He didn't even have a photo to help him with identification. He would need to call Audrey at the chalets. If he was staying there he may have left an address. He picked up the phone and dialed her number.

"The Three Suites, Audrey speaking," she sang into the phone.

"Constable Driver here. We have a situation you may be able to help us with," he paused. "A car has gone over the cliff on Radar Hill and it appears to belong to a Mr. John Campbell. I have been told he was a guest at your chalets." He waited for her response.

There was quite a silence before Audrey said "John Campbell. You said?"

"Yes. I was wondering if you had an address or credit card receipt. We need to locate his family."

"Is he dead?" asked Audrey.

"No, well we don't know for sure. He is officially missing at this time," he said. "We do need to contact his family. Can you give me his address?"

Audrey paused then said, "I am so sorry Constable but he called by phone to make the reservation and paid in cash when he arrived."

"Don't you require a deposit or credit card information to hold a booking?" he asked frustrated.

"He only called a day or so before and he sounded like a business man. I didn't worry about it."

"Did he leave a phone number?" he asked.

She said. "No. But you can ask Captain Todd. He went out on a fishing trip with him on the day he left. He may have paid him by credit card or left a phone number."

"He never turned up for the trip," said Driver. "I saw his car parked down by the dock. But there was no sign of the man."

"I am so sorry," said Audrey apologetically. "If I remember anything that may help I will call you."

"So you say he checked out on Saturday morning to go on the fishing trip and you haven't seen him since?" he asked.

"That's right," she said. He must have checked out very early because his car was gone when I woke up."

"Thanks," said Driver. "I will be sending a sketch artist over to you shortly. I would appreciate it if you could assist with a likeness of the man. You are the only person to have seen him and I would like to get the sketch on the six o'clock news tonight." He went on to get a brief description of the man over the phone.

"Late fifties, good looking, greyish hair, good physique, about six feet tall," she provided.

The team had called in to say they had done a complete search of the area and no body was found. They had even searched deep in the forest behind where the car had been found with no success. The car had been completely gone over. Apart from a few maps in the glove compartment there was no sign of a cell phone, wallet, computer or anything personal left in the car except for his clothing, golf clubs and fishing gear. It was as if the man had simply disappeared and didn't want to be found.

Driver felt as soon as they could track down his family and friends they may have the answer to the man's disappearance. Maybe there were money troubles, women troubles or legal troubles. Something must have made Mr. John Campbell want to push his car off a cliff and disappear. Did he want it to look like an accident? Was it murder? He would have to involve the local and national newspapers. He would also arrange an interview on the six o'clock news. He picked up the phone and made the necessary phone calls. Someone must know a John Campbell who had taken a fishing trip to Northland. Someone would know who he was.

Chapter 64

Pearl never missed the six o'clock news. She nearly jumped out of her chair when she saw Constable Driver on the news again. This time talking about another man who had gone missing in Whangaroa. "Shit!" she said to the little dog sitting on the sofa beside her "another one." She listened while the constable went on to say a car was found over the cliff on Radar Hill. "The car's registration shows it belongs to a Mr. John Campbell. It would appear the driver of the car has gone missing. We would like to talk to anyone who knows of a John Campbell, late 50s, who drives a black 4runner license plate Number MS3047 and had planned a fishing trip to Whangaroa." The Constable was holding up a sketch of the missing man. "He stayed at a local lodge on Friday night and went missing on Saturday. If anyone has any information please contact your local police department."

That was it. Pearl couldn't sit down. She paced up and down her little TV room. Her mind was racing. Two men missing and they both stayed at Audrey's. They found the bones of one man. What was going on?

He had mentioned a fishing trip. She called the local club and asked who was the skipper of the boat John Campbell was booked on. She found out it was her friend, Old Todd. She called him but he was no use. He said the man hadn't turned up on Saturday morning. He left messages at the chalet, but no-one called him back.

"Gone missing, they say," said Todd. "They found his car over Radar Hill but no sign of the man. Wouldn't be any big deal except the other guy's car was also in a strange accident. Something is going on."

Pearl agreed and made another call immediately. She would get to the bottom of this.

Audrey answered the phone. It was Pearl.

"Can you believe it? Who was he? You met him. What was he like? Was he depressed? Do you think it was suicide?" Pearl blurted into the phone.

"I can't talk now," said Audrey. "I have someone here. I will call you later." She hung the phone.

Audrey had a visitor. He was sitting outside on her patio smoking a cigarette. He looked so handsome in his cowboy hat, checkered shirt and jeans. She had convinced him to have a glass of wine with her. He said he didn't really drink but obliged anyway and took off his hat ready to stay awhile.

She walked back outside carrying two glasses of her best wine. She wished she could have a ciggy but knew just one puff would set her off again. Harry had been telling her about the pigs he had shot the night before. "They were big buggers," he had said. "Two big boars with huge tusks." He wanted to go back again tonight at dark to catch the rest. "There are at least four others," he said. "I saw a big sow and her weaners. They look as though they have been there for some time. Why didn't you get me to shoot them before?"

"I didn't want to have guns going off around the guests," Audrey said shyly.

She wondered if Harry found her attractive. She was older than him. *By at least five years*, she thought. His wife had looked at least ten years younger than her and much prettier. She found herself blushing when Harry looked at her. She felt he knew about the dream she had of him the night before. It had completely changed her demeanor. She found herself being flirty and funny. She wanted to please him and encouraged him to talk about his ex-wife and the divorce and how lonely he had been since she left him a year ago. She was soothing and comforting and listened sympathetically.

She invited him to dinner the next night and maybe a hot tub too. "A good home cooked meal is what you need," she said. Harry seemed painfully shy around her. He said he would like to come to dinner. He put on his hat and returned to his quad bike and dog, parked on the gravel driveway.

Audrey hadn't watched the six o'clock news she was too busy flirting with Harry. She had recorded the show so she sat down to watch it now. She listened while Constable Driver talked about John Campbell.

They will never find him, she thought. *He was a wanker. He deserved everything he got*. She turned off the TV and sat thinking about what she was going to cook for dinner tomorrow night. It was going to be a special night. A few drinks, a hot tub, dancing in the moonlight. It had been such a long time since she had felt like being romantic. She had Harry Armstrong to thank for that.

Chapter 65

The calls started coming in as soon as the news spot on Campbell was over. First it was a guy called Jimmy from a Beer Distributing company. He said John Campbell was his boss. He had no idea where he might be or why his 4runner was found over a cliff. He was taking a holiday to celebrate he was turning the company over to him. John was going to retire. He was really happy to have time now to fish and play golf. No, he was not suicidal. No, he wasn't married. He had two ex-wives. Yes, he would be available to talk to the police tomorrow. No, he didn't think he was traveling with anyone else or planning to meet up with anyone up north.

Next it was one of John Campbell's 'girls.' She said her name was Delia. She had seen him a few nights ago. He was looking forward to his trip up north. No, she didn't know if he knew anyone up by Kaeo or Whangaroa. She had never been up there. She said he was a nice man. She told Driver he had been married twice before but it was a long time ago. She said he preferred his 'girls' to a relationship. She had been one of his clients for many years. He was not depressed, she said. He seemed like a happy go lucky guy although he was terribly anal-retentive. Liked everything neat and tidy.

Calls kept on coming all the next day. Ex-wives, girls of the night, employees, work colleagues and old school mates.

Driver looked at his notes. He made a check mark next to Jimmy's name. Maybe Jimmy and John Campbell had a misunderstanding about the take-over. Maybe John had no intention of retiring and Jimmy preferred to have him gone what ever it took. He needed to check up on it.

He couldn't imagine any of his ex-wives or lovers or girlfriends would want him gone. They all seemed pretty fond of the guy. "Nice Guy" was what he heard over and over again.

It was more likely John Campbell's problems started when he came to Whangaroa. But who wanted him gone? He went back to his list of comparisons and added to his list. Both men stayed at The Three Suites and Audrey was the last person to see both men alive.

They needed to complete their search of Audrey's property. He would get the team back up there today. This time they would do another, more detailed, search of Suite C. Maybe John Campbell had left something behind in the room. But knowing Audrey, she would have cleaned his room the moment he left. Cleaned and then cleaned again. Any trace of either man would have been scrubbed and washed away by now. If Suite C was the crime scene they would never had known. Both men had not been reported missing. In fact, no-one knew they were missing until their vehicles were found. They had both dined down in Whangaroa and then returned to spend their last night in Suite C. Audrey had heard their cars leave the next morning. What happened to them after they left the chalets? Did someone stop them on the road? Were they robbed, killed and their cars pushed over a cliff?

Driver picked up the phone and organized the search. They would spend all day there if they had to. It was the last location both men had been seen alive.

Chapter 66

Audrey was singing. She hadn't sung in years. Today she was going to drive into Kerikeri to the supermarket and pick up what she needed for dinner tonight. While she was there she would shop for a new outfit. Kerikeri was a good thirty-five minutes drive and most stores closed early on Sunday. Or didn't open at all. Audrey lived in a constant state of fashion uncertainty. She was born a middle child in a working class family and never developed her own fashion identity. Her wardrobe belonged to her two older sisters. Any hand made dress was made unison in design and only separated by color. Her color was always pink. A color she has disliked with an intensity in her grown-up years. Her body shape fluctuated from fit and slender to full and robust. Usually she hated the way she looked and was shocked when she glimpsed her reflection in a store window.

Once she was with her sister in London running to catch a bus. A nice-looking gentleman at the bus stop commented excitedly, "You are Dolly Parton."

Audrey couldn't help but laugh. He was absolutely right. She did look like Dolly Parton.

Mostly she felt a stranger in her own body. Years of dieting had left her metabolism in tatters along with her self-esteem. She would shop constantly trying to find a garment that would satisfy her urge to be someone else. Today would be no different. She would return with something new only to be forgotten by tomorrow and lost in her overstuffed wardrobe. But tonight was all she could think about. She chose her usual jeans and topped it with a tailored black jacket and black boots and headed out the door.

As she drove down the driveway she was passed by what seemed like the whole country's police force. Cars started streaming up the driveway filled with uniformed men.

Constable Driver stopped and talked to her. "We are just finishing off the property search," he said. "We were interrupted the other day. Are you going out?"

"Yes', said Audrey "I am going into Kerikeri for a few hours. I am guessing you don't need me around?"

"No, no, go ahead," he said. "But first, can I have a set of keys for the suites. We have a warrant to search the whole property and we just want to make sure we have covered everything before we go."

Audrey passed a set of Master keys through the car window to him. "No worries. There are no guests checking in today," she said as she started to drive away. "I will be back in a couple of hours or so."

On her drive through the Northland rural countryside she thought about what the police may find. Nothing, they will find nothing. She had covered everything including the small carry bag she had sitting in her back seat. She needed to dispose of its contents and she knew exactly the place to do it. Somewhere the police had never searched and with somebody they hadn't even suspected. She took a turn to the right and headed up Old Hospital road. She passed the Community Hospital on her right where the road was unsealed and rough. Only a few miles up the road she stopped and parked her car off the road, where it was hidden, down an old driveway. She would walk the rest of the way through the scrub and bush so she wouldn't be seen by anyone passing by.

She changed into her gumboots and picked up the black carry bag and headed across the grassy paddocks towards an old broken down bungalow.

She stood behind some bushes and watched. She saw him walk out of the front door to his motorbike. The yard was strewn with old cars and bike parts. She knew he made deliveries on Sunday morning to his regulars. She despised the man. Not because he was a drug dealer but because he was a member of the Black Power gang. She had heard he had been involved in a gang rape of a woman years ago. She was brutally raped by fifteen members of his gang. He was never jailed. He was also a suspect in the crime against the previous Kaeo cop who had his head bashed in. She watched as he put on his black helmet and swung his leg over the bike. She knew she could finally get justice for his crime and, at the same time, get Driver off her case. He would have bigger problems once it became common knowledge that his wife was involved.

The biker took off in a cloud of dust and Audrey stepped out of her hiding place and went over to where his old truck was parked. She was wearing gloves and had made sure her hair was completely covered. She didn't want to leave any of her DNA.

She knew he used the truck for hauling his auto parts to and from customers. The door was open and she climbed inside. She found the perfect place to store her bag's contents. She opened the glove compartment and saw a small plastic bag of weed tucked in the back. She removed the bag along with a dirty envelope containing an unpaid electric bill and tucked them in her pocket.

Audrey had been keeping watch on the biker for a while now. She couldn't believe her luck when she had spotted Driver's wife in disguise knocking at his front door. The discovery she was a druggy combined with the biker's past reputation made them perfect scapegoats for her planned events. She had already removed Dolly and Bruce's letterbox and made the anonymous donation to the biker. It wouldn't be long before someone spotted it proudly perched atop his front gate.

With her task completed Audrey returned to her car and continued on her way to buy her wine, fruit, veges and a leg of lamb. Hopefully the dress shop was still open. Dinner was going to wonderful and she was going to look stunning.

Chapter 67

Pearl saw them. There must have been at least five cop cars heading up Wainui Road. *Where are they going?* thought Pearl. *Have they found the body?* She called Audrey but just got her answer phone. She called Smithy but there was no answer. *Damn.* They didn't have their sirens on so it must not have been an emergency. She pondered.

She liked to go to church. Not because she was religious but because it was an opportunity to catch up on gossip. The community was not separated by Pakeha and Maori but by druggies and God-lovers. Pearl never took drugs but liked her wine and quite a lot of it. She passed out most nights with a glass in her hand only to awaken at some ungodly hour before the rest of the world stirred. This morning she was wearing her sequin cowboy dress and boots. She had tied a tasseled scarf around her hips and was feeling rather proud of her appearance.

Church was held in a wonderful little wooden church, still standing from the days of the missionaries, who were early settlers in Kaeo. Pearl knew everyone in the church. Well, almost everyone. Today Constable Driver's family was in church. Pearl thought they looked like a nice family. The two young boys were about ten years old and Mrs. Driver was a nice looking lady. After the service they all congregated outside on the green lawn. The topic of conversation was the two missing men. Everyone had his or her opinion. No-one could decide on one, single culprit. What they were unanimous about, was murder.

"No question it was murder," said a local schoolteacher. "How else can you explain the fact the cars were involved in an accident, but no bodies were found near the site?"

Many of the residents blamed drugs. Druggies need money, that they agreed upon. After all, neither of the guys' wallets were found.

Pearl racked her brains during her trip back home. If it was murder for drug money, she worried her son's gang was involved. He was a member of the Black Power gang. She had never approved of his gang affiliations, but he was always a trouble-maker and Pearl had nothing to do with him since he became a member.

The gang had a strong foothold in the area. And if they were involved, chances were, they would never be brought to justice. There were just too many of them and proving it would be almost impossible.

Pearl didn't feel like going home yet. She decided to go for a drive up by her son's house. She hadn't been there for years. Although they only lived about ten minutes from each other it was her way of saying she didn't approve of his new life. She slowed down as she approached her son's house. Then she saw it, Dolly and Bruce's letterbox proudly sitting atop her son's gate. Bruce had told her their letterbox was stolen and she was shocked her son would take it. After all, it was just a letterbox and everyone in the town knew the yellow painted little house letterbox belonged to Dolly and Bruce. She didn't stop but did a u-turn further up the road and headed home. Maybe her son was sending a message to Dolly and Bruce. She suspected he was their drug supplier. Maybe they owed him money and he was sending some sort of message. She returned home and made herself a nice cup of tea. "Nothing like a cup of tea to make you feel better," she said to her little dog, that came excitedly to the door to greet her.

Chapter 68

They had been there a couple of hours searching inside the suites and the surrounding area. As they headed up into the pine forest behind the chalets the dogs started barking and pulling at their leads. The police let the two dogs off their leads and the group followed them up the dirt track to a large green water tank. The dogs were sniffing around the tank and then ran further up the track to where Audrey had planted her vegetable garden. The cops could smell something dead. One of the dogs had stopped in his tracks. It was a dead possum. The other dog started sniffing around the garden. The police saw where pigs had rooted up the ground. It appeared they had caught something around here. There was lamb's wool stuck to a couple of the branches. "Wild pigs have obviously got one of the sheep," said Driver. They continued their search as the dogs gave every indication there had definitely been a kill or two here. "I'll go and ask Armstrong if he knows about any wild pigs up here," said Driver. "He is an avid pig hunter, I hear."

"Good idea" said one of the detectives. "This garden looks

pretty new. Why would the lady make a garden up here in the woods? Do you think we should dig it up?"

"Lets organize a small digger to excavate the whole area tomorrow" said Driver. "I'll go and find Armstrong," he added as he headed on foot down the hill to his car.

Driver found Armstrong in the cow shed. He was finishing off the day's milking. Driver didn't want to disturb him so waited by the turn gate for the last cow to leave the shed. The cows all walked quietly towards their paddock relieved of the extra weight they had been carrying. Armstrong waved to him and, when he had closed the gate behind the herd, walked back to where Driver was waiting.

"We are hoping you can help us," said Driver. "Do you have a minute or two?"

"Yep," said Armstrong wiping his hands on his coveralls. "What do you need?"

"Would you come over the chalets with me. We have a situation over there and need some advise."

"Sure" he replied. "Can you wait a moment while I hose off the yard?"

"No problem," said Driver. As he watched the farmer working. he felt a slight envy for his lifestyle devoid of crime.

"I will follow you over on my bike. I have to check some cattle over that way," said Harry. He jumped on his bike and followed the police car back to the chalets.

They both parked by Suite C and headed up the hill on foot. Driver asked him if he had seen any wild pigs around Audrey's place. "I shot a couple of them last night for her," he said. "She had planted a garden up there and found her pet lamb dead. I got rid of the lamb and shot the pigs for her. Caught a couple beauties. I told her I would get the rest tonight. They have been making a mess up there."

Driver asked him why she hadn't got him to shoot the pigs before.

"She doesn't like anyone pig hunting on her property while guests are staying there. I guess she has no bookings for the next couple of days and so this is a good time to get rid of them," he answered.

When they reached the site, Driver noticed the police were searching the area thoroughly.

"Found anything?" he asked. "Nothing yet," said the detective. "But the dogs can definitely smell death here."

"This is Harry Armstrong," introduced Driver. "He's the farmer next door and a well-known pig shooter in the area. At least, that is what Old Smithy says."

Harry walked over to where Audrey had planted her garden and showed where he had seen the pigs the night before. "Mean buggers," he said. "I am guessing there are at least two, possibly more, up here. I am coming back at dark tonight to get the last of them. Hopefully my dogs will sniff them out."

"Would they attack a man?" asked Driver feeling rather ignorant where wild pigs are concerned.

"Not unless he was passed out or injured. But I can't imagine anyone would be wandering around up here. The chalets are a fairly busy place and Audrey keeps a strict eye on things here."

"Thanks," said Driver. "You say you will be back here tonight? Let us know if you see anything unusual."

"Will do," said Harry as he started back down the hill to his bike.

Chapter 69

S*trange,* thought Harry. *Why would the police be so interested in pig infestation? Do they think it was wild pigs that killed the two missing men? But why would their bodies be so far away from their cars*? He was beginning to have second thoughts about accepting the dinner invitation from Audrey. He only agreed to come to dinner to be neighborly after all. He didn't really find Audrey an attractive lady. She was much too old and too buxom for him. He preferred his ladies young, small and petite. For the past year he had been a regular in the Whangaroa brothel scene although he never actually visited the brothels. He preferred private visits and had two regular girls he saw on Tuesday and Thursday nights. He enjoyed the routine of getting dressed up in his best jeans and a clean shirt and knowing he was going to get laid.

Sex was important to Harry. His ex-wife had been very sexual and he wished he could afford more visits out of town. He liked to buy a full hour of their time. It felt more civilized and romantic than simply paying for a bonk by the minute.

Harry was quite a romantic man although his shyness around

women made it difficult to approach them. His Tuesday and Thursday women drained his bank account but provided what he needed. His farm kept him busy and he was already losing acreage to his ex- wife, along with a heavy financial settlement. It meant a huge mortgage on his farm, which he had finally made freehold of debt only a couple of years before.

Harry moved the cattle from the flats below to a couple of paddocks behind Smithy's old house. Smithy was out burning some trash and creating a nasty black, poisonous smoke trail into the blue sky. Harry stopped and asked him what he was burning.

"Just some upholstery out of the old cars," said Smithy who had a collection of car parts scattered across his property.

"Smells more like old tires," said Harry knowing that was exactly what he was burning, illegally. "Watch the cops across the road don't smell it," said Harry.

"Oh shit?" said Smithy. "Better put it out. What are the cops doing up at Audrey's again?" he asked. "They seem to be spending a lot of time there."

"They are checking out the pa area. They are concerned about the wild pigs. I guess they think the pigs may have had something to do with the bones found at the bottom of the valley."

Harry left Smithy to put out his fire and headed on back to feed his pigs and check on the sheep. Maybe I will telephone Audrey and say I am too busy on the farm to have dinner but I will go up and shoot the pigs later, when it gets dark.

Chapter 70

Audrey was exhausted. She must have tried on at least twenty different outfits. She hated trying on clothes. She had to look in the huge mirror in the dressing room and they all made you look fatter than you really were. She squeezed into sizes obviously too small for her. Nothing fit over her boobs. Then, finally, she found a long black top that didn't look too bad. She forgot she owned at least three similar tops but it was all about having something new for tonight. 'New' made her feel more special somehow. Her stripy black skirt would work wonderfully with the top. Now she had to get back to the chalets and wash her hair and get the roast lamb in the oven. She hoped the cops had all left. She didn't need them hanging around spoiling her good mood.

It was almost three-thirty before she arrived back home. She didn't realize how long she had been in Kerikeri. As she pulled up the driveway she noticed all the police cars were gone. She breathed a sigh of relief "Thank goodness," she said.

She unloaded her groceries and put the wine in the fridge to chill. She prepared the leg of lamb with fresh rosemary and little slithers of garlic pushed into freshly cut slits in the skin of the lamb. She poured over olive oil, added a sprinkle of salt and pepper and put the pan in the oven set at 375 deg. She peeled kumara, potatoes, pumpkin, parsnips and onions and cut them to size and placed them in a large bowl of water ready to just pop in the oven in an hour or so. Then she went upstairs and took a long shower. She didn't hear the phone ringing downstairs. She was oblivious to anything other than her thoughts of a wonderful evening.

She was in love. She knew she was finally in that wonderful place that lovers go. Everything looked brighter, more alive. She had put the vegetables in the over half an hour ago and the aroma of a roast dinner in the oven permeated throughout the suite.

She poured herself a glass of wine. It was five-thirty. Dinner would be ready in about an hour. She had told Harry to come at six thirty. She still had to cook the peas and make the gravy. She had already made the mint sauce with fresh mint from her garden.

She sipped her wine and checked the temperature of the hot tub. It was perfect. Tonight was going to be a special night. Full of romance, laughter and, if she was lucky, he might even make a pass at her. She did look lovely in her new black top and pencil skirt.

At six thirty she put on her favorite music - Keb Mo and listened for the quad bike. She imagined he would be on the quad bike because he would be going up to shoot the pigs when it got dark. The dogs would need to be tied up while they had dinner or they may smell the pigs and take off up the mountain. She looked at the clock again. The peas and gravy were cooked. She had turned down the oven so the lamb and vegetables would not overcook. Everything was perfect. She had set the table for two with soft green tablemats and matching napkins and picked flowers out of her garden to create a nice centerpiece. Two wine glasses sat empty in anticipation of the evening.

It was almost seven o'clock. Audrey was worried about the dinner. Soon it would become overcooked. There was nothing Audrey hated more than overcooked food. It reminded her of her Mother's cooking when she was a child.

Her happy mood was beginning to get darker and darker. She was always early for an appointment. Lateness was a sign of rudeness and Audrey couldn't tolerate it. She picked up the phone to call Harry. Maybe he had a problem on the farm.

Then she heard it... the familiar message tone, beep...beep... beep.... "Damn," she said "It better not be Harry to say he isn't coming." She hadn't thought to check for messages. She keyed in her code:

"Hey Audrey," she heard. "It's Harry here. Sorry, but I can't make dinner tonight – too busy on the farm. But don't worry I will still take care of the pigs. I will be up there when it gets dark about nine thirty or so. I won't disturb you. So sorry about the dinner, but just too busy at the moment."

Audrey threw the phone across the room. It hit the wall and shattered. "Fucking Men!" she screamed. "I hate them! Selfish, lying bastards!" She knew Harry just didn't want to come to dinner. Didn't want to spend any time with her. "I bet he sleeps with hussies. Filthy, dirty, disgusting, fucking men!" she shouted as she took the dinner out of the oven and threw it into the trash bins outside her suite. The peas, gravy and mint sauce she poured down the sink. "Wasted! Wasted! Wasted! All of it wasted!"

Audrey huddled into a ball on the floor in the corner of the room. She hugged her knees, put her head in her lap and cried. "I tried," she said. "I tried to be nice." They all hate me and I hate them. Their dirty penises, groping hands, filthy mouths," she sobbed.

Then Audrey knew what she must do. She sat on the floor and made a plan. Finally she stood up, found her glass of wine, turned off the music, cleaned the kitchen, picked up the broken phone and changed into her sweat pants and sweat top. She filled her glass for the third time and sat quietly on her patio in the evening air.

In half an hour she would take a quick trip to Kaeo. She had a little chore to do. She knew Constable Driver and his family would go down to the Waterfront Restaurant for the Sunday night Roast Dinner. He had mentioned it the other day to her and while they were out. She had a little gift she wanted to deliver.

Chapter 71

Harry sat down to his dinner. He had cooked up a few pork chops and mashed some spuds. It may not be as good as Audrey's dinner but at least he didn't have to try and make conversation. He was not a social animal. Pig hunting, farming and sex was about all he cared about and not particularly in that order. He turned on the evening news. They were still talking about the missing men in Whangaroa. The police were following certain leads but the cases were not considered homicides and yet they could not confirm them as accidents until further investigations were made. "The second man had not been found and was now confirmed missing," the announcer said. Harry thought about the last person to see them alive. It was Audrey. Both men had stayed at the chalets before they went missing. The police obviously suspected something or they wouldn't be spending so much time up there. *They should be checking out some the gang members around here*, he thought. *They are a dangerous lot.*

As he watched the rest of the news he became more and more

relaxed. Before long he had fallen asleep on the sofa. It was almost nine o'clock when he awoke.

He looked up at the old clock on the wall. He lived in his Mother's house. She had passed away a short time ago. It was his Mum and Dad's house for many years. His Dad had it built when he was just a small boy. It was about forty years old now but still in good nick. Harry had been running the farm since his father died. The family had a good reputation in the area. The Maori Marae was next door, surrounded by a small Maori settlement. Some of the youth were Black Power members. But most of the Maori in the area were nice folk. Many of them remembered Harry's Mum and Dad and were fond of Harry. Harry's sons and daughters were not interested in running the farm. He wondered, when he died what would happen to the farm. He guessed it would have to be sold to pay off the mortgage.

Harry was looking forward to some pig hunting. He went into his bedroom and changed into some old jeans and a thick cotton shirt. The sleep had given him more energy and he felt revived. Pig hunting really got your adrenalin pumping. The dogs would find the pigs and grab them, waiting for Harry to get close enough for a shot.

The night air felt good. Harry drove up the pa and through the top gate into Audrey's property. His lights lit up the forest. He turned them off and slowed down as he reached the new garden plot. He climbed off the bike and let the dogs go. It wasn't long before he could hear squealing and barking. He ran expertly through the forest and caught up with the dogs. They had caught a big one and had it held by the ears. Harry took aim and shot it right between the eyes. It fell to the ground instantly. He cut its throat, pulled it downhill towards his bike and, with all his might, he lifted it onto the front grill. The dogs took off again and he followed them. They had another one. His aim was perfect. He dragged the second pig down the hill to the dirt track. He would need to come back for this one. The dogs were excited. They liked pig hunting as much as he did. Harry and the dogs headed back to the farm. He would return later for the other pig. He still needed to feed all the dogs and put these two in their kennels.

Chapter 72

Audrey parked her car in a side road in the shadows and walked through the back of the petrol station to the police station. She had dressed in her masculine disguise, hiding her hair in a woolen hat and had pulled up the hood of her sweatshirt. She wore gumboots which were non-gender and worn by most of the locals. If anyone saw her, they definitely wouldn't recognize her.

She let herself in the through the back laundry door. No one ever locked his or her back doors in Kaeo. Everybody mistakenly thought it a safe area. It used to be but times were changing in the small town. She turned on her headlight and walked from room to room. They had unpacked almost everything. She had to find somewhere that was obviously his wife's but he had regular access to it. She didn't have too long, they would be back from dinner soon.

Then she saw the perfect place. His police jacket was hanging on the hook by the back door. He had quickly hung it over his wife's winter jacket. She carefully placed the small plastic bag, with the illegal contents and the electric bill, in between both jackets. When he removed his jacket the bag would fall to the ground. Leaving unanswered questions and an address to call on.

Audrey made it back to the chalets in time to hear the first shot. Her anger hadn't subsided, but rather escalated during the last couple of hours. She poured herself another wine. She sat outside on the patio in the darkness listening to Harry and the dogs. She heard a second shot. He had got both pigs. A short time later she heard him drive back across the top of the hill towards his farm. She walked up the hill to where the dead boar lay on the track. He was huge. There was blood dripping out of his mouth. "You are an ugly one," said Audrey as she looked down at the gruesome site. She turned and walked back down to her suite to wait for the sound of Harry's bike returning.

She felt a certain sense of satisfaction knowing Constable Driver and his family would be returning from their happy family dinner. She knew he would not be reaching for his jacket this evening. Tomorrow morning would be just fine. She needed to divert his focus away from her and to where it should belong.

He was back. She had changed into her sexiest jeans tucked now into her gumboots. She made her way back up the hill and met him by the dead boar.

"I heard the shots," said Audrey. "Wonderful. Thanks so much. It was really quite scary having them so close to the chalets. Let me offer you a drink to say thank you" she said sweetly.

"I'm sorry I couldn't get the time to come to dinner," he said.

"Oh, don't even think about it. You poor man, you must be so busy running the farm all by yourself," she said. "I do have a wonderful apple sponge hot and in the oven. Come on down. That pig is not going anywhere." And before he could say no, she had turned and headed back down the hill. She was pleased she hadn't thrown away the apple sponge. It was perfect bait for any man. All men loved their mother's cooking and home cooked apple sponge was any son's favorite.

They sat outside on the patio. It was a warm evening. She lit a candle and placed it in the center of the table. There was no breeze and the flame flickered softly, providing a romantic ambiance to their surroundings.

She opened a bottle of her favorite: Stoneleigh Sauvignon Blanc and passed a glass to Harry.

"Thanks," he said noncommittally.

She brought out two bowls of the pudding "Would you like some cream on yours?" she asked softly.

"Yes, please," he said.

She handed him the cream jug and they sat in silence enjoying the warm pudding.

Audrey looked at the man sitting in front of her. Maybe she had been too quick to jump to conclusions. Before she poured his second glass of wine she would give him a second chance. He finished his desert and lit up a smoke.

"Nice night," he said trying desperately to make conversation.

Audrey asked him, "So are you seeing anyone?"

"What do you mean?" he said.

"Do you have a girlfriend?" she explained.

"Oh no. I don't have much time for that," he looked a little put off by such a direct question.

"Yes it is hard dating again after you go through a divorce," she said. "It took me quite a while before I could even think about being with another man."

Harry looked awkward and changed the subject "Did the cops find anything during their search today" he enquired.

"I have no idea. They were gone when I got back.

Though obviously not, or Constable Driver would have telephoned me."

"What were the two guys like?" Harry asked.

"Just nice, ordinary guys," said Audrey. "Nothing special. You know, fishing and golfing types." She tried to bring the conversation back to them. "So what do you do for fun?" she asked.

"Oh you know, pig hunting mostly. My farm keeps me pretty busy," he said.

Audrey tried again "I hear they have dancing down at the waterfront some Saturday nights. Do you like to dance?"

"Nah. Never danced much" he replied. He stood up ready to go "Well thanks for the apple sponge. It was great. I've gotta go. Still have to take the pig back and I have to get up early in the morning. Thanks Audrey."

He didn't want her. She could tell. He couldn't wait to get away. It was now or never. "Please stay for another glass of wine," she said. "I could really do with the company. All this has been so stressful on me. Just one more glass," she pleaded.

"Sorry Audrey, "I really have to get going."

Audrey remained seated at the table and watched as he took large strides up the grassy bank to his quad bike. She heard him lift the last remaining pig onto the bike and drive away into the darkness.

"He is not going anywhere," she muttered. "There is plenty of time." Her day had started with such high expectations and now she was left to clear away the remnants of the night's disappointments.

Chapter 73

Monday morning and the boys were still not dressed for school. Maria had decided to drop the boys off and then head off down to Kerikeri. She wanted to enroll them into one of the schools there. She had heard the Kerikeri School had a good reputation and she needed to organize their transfer. She had made porridge for breakfast with brown sugar and cream. The boys loved that. Her husband liked it too. She was coping a lot better now she had her supply of weed. She had to be so careful not to smoke it around Dennis. She would go out behind the house to an empty paddock and take a few puffs whenever she got a chance.

Her husband sat at the table and joined them all for breakfast. They liked to eat breakfast together. Often it was the only meal they shared all day. Driver looked at his watch. Seven-thirty all ready. He must call Carl, the local digger driver, and get him up to Audrey's garden site and start digging. He kissed his wife goodbye and headed towards the front door. He swooped up his jacket and something fell to the floor. He bent down to pick it up. It took him a moment to figure out what it was. He opened the little plastic bag and, sure enough, it was weed. He looked on the floor and saw that a piece of paper had fallen down with it. He looked at it closely. It was a bill of some kind addressed to Hemi Heke, 396 Old Hospital Road, Kaeo.

"Hey Maria," he called to his wife. "Come here."

Maria walked around the corner and saw her husband holding a small bag and a small torn piece of paper in his hand. She knew what it was immediately. But it was not hers. She had kept hers hidden in a sock in her bottom drawer.

"What is it?" she asked.

"It's weed," said Driver. "It fell out of your coat."

"No way," she said. "It is not mine. See it has an address on it." And then she gasped. It was the name of her supplier. Shit! He would kill her if her husband arrived on his doorstep. It wouldn't take long for him to work out it was her who brought this on him.

"What do you know about this?" he asked looking at her straight in the eyes. She didn't waver.

"Someone must have put it there," she explained. "I have no idea."

Driver put the weed and the paper in his pocket and headed out the door. He didn't even stop to check messages at the station. He got straight into his car and headed out to old Hospital Road.

When he arrived at the address on the note he noticed the Dolly and Bruce's yellow letterbox was on the gate. At least it was a letterbox like Dolly had described to him, a yellow little house with a painted red roof. He saw a motorbike parked in the driveway and a truck. He had radioed in the name and address on the way and he was told Hemi Heke was a Black Power Gang member and had been suspected of dealing drugs in the past.

He decided to get back up and radioed to the Kerikeri

station. Driver was pissed off. If this guy supplied his wife with weed he was going down. There was nothing like a drug bust to get your adrenalin pumping. He parked further up the road where he could keep a watch. It was still early He doubted if anyone would be up and about this early. He waited for the others to arrive. It was a good half hour drive.

He needed a good arrest on his record. Auckland was already questioning their decision to send him to Kaeo. He had two men missing. One obviously dead, the other missing and no arrests or even suspects brought in for questioning. He needed this bust.

As Driver sat and waiting in his car his thoughts went back to Maria's expression when she saw the address on the paper. She knew something. He just knew it. She must be taking dope again? She used to take it when they first met. In fact, they both used to smoke it now and then. Once Driver joined the police force, all that was over. He has suspected she was still doing it. He really didn't want to know, so he never asked. He hoped this incident would scare the living daylights out of her. He could lose his job if his wife is keeping dope in their house. It had to stop.

He saw them arrive. They parked behind him and together they stormed the house.

Chapter 74

Audrey had spent a restless night and awoke late morning. Last night she just couldn't get to sleep and when she finally did, she kept dreaming about Harry. Why was he in such a hurry to leave last night? Why wouldn't he stay awhile? Audrey had wanted to share a hot tub with him. Get close to him. *Well, Fuck him!* she thought. It was Monday and she didn't feel like going anywhere or talking to anyone. She would keep the curtains drawn and watch movies all day. Maybe later she would go for a drive and see if the little gift she left the constable was appreciated.

Still in her dressing gown, Audrey climbed the hill to the new garden plot. The plants were doing well. She dragged over the garden hose and gave everything a good watering. There were marks over the track where Harry had dragged the pigs last night. She could see drops of blood still left on the ground. Audrey may not have graduated high school but she certainly wasn't stupid. She had obviously outsmarted the police and their dogs.

At noon she made herself a nice cup of tea and sat down to watch a little telly. There was a news flash. A police helicopter was circling over a house in Kaeo not far from the Community Hospital. The reporter announced, "A black power gang member had been arrested and is being charged with drug possession and murder. The police had found articles belonging to both missing men on his premises along with a large supply of marijuana and methamphetamine. He was being held without bail. We will keep on top of the story and report updates as they are received."

Audrey's black mood lifted immediately. She felt like celebrating. "They caught him. They caught him," she sang. "He cannot wriggle out of this one. This time he will go to jail. Shithead! Rapist! Druggy! Mister you deserve everything that's coming to you."

Her phone started ringing. "The Three Suites. Audrey speaking."

It was Pearl in tears "Oh Audrey. Did you hear? It was my son who did it."

"No" said Audrey. "I just watched the news it was a Black Power gang member."

"He is my son," said Pearl. "No-one really knew because we haven't been close for many years. This is awful. I knew he was into drugs - but murder? I didn't think he was capable of killing anyone. I wonder if Dolly and Bruce were involved too?" she sobbed. "I saw their letterbox at Hemi's house and they are big time druggies. I wouldn't be surprised if they dumped the vehicles. I have to go to the police station. Constable Driver wants to talk to me." Pearl confided tearfully. "They wont let me talk to Hemi. They said he is in custody and can have no visitors while they are interrogating him. Oh, Audrey can you come with me?" She pleaded. "I don't want to go alone."

She lied. "I am so sorry Pearl, but I have guests checking in any moment now and I can't leave the chalets. What about Marge at the pub? I am sure she will go with you."

"Ok," said Pearl, "I'll call her. This is terrible." The phone clicked.

The town would be buzzing with the news. Hemi Heke, the Black Power gang member arrested for murder. Audrey made herself another cup of tea and put a movie into the DVD. The afternoon was going to be wonderful. Shame she threw the leg of lamb in the rubbish tin. A nice lamb sandwich would go down well right now.

THE END

ALSO BY LEONIE MATEER

THE AUDREY MURDERS – BOOK SERIES

The Murder Suite —Book One

The Cabin by the Sea — Book Two

The Murder Trail — Book Three

Murder in the Family — Book Four

The Murder Trap — Book Five

Murder in Lockdown — Book Six

The Taupo Bay Killings — Book Seven

If you enjoyed this book, I would be so appreciative if you would write a brief review on Amazon. Thank you.

Leonie Mateer

www.leoniemateer.com

About the Author

Puppeteer, children's entertainer, model agency owner, TV talk show panelist, luxury accommodation owner, entrepreneur, product developer, brand developer, storyteller, author, and indie publisher Leonie Mateer has lived a full and diverse life.

Born and raised in New Zealand, Mateer moved to the United States in her thirties to pursue business opportunities. She returned to New Zealand for several years in the 2000s, running a luxury lodge in Northland—which has been an inspiration for her crime series—and now splits her time between Northland, New Zealand, and the United States.

Mateer is known for her huge success as a brand development expert. She received 'Who's Who' awards from both Leading American Executives and American Inventors in the 1990s. As the creator of the brand Caboodles™, a teen girl brand that took the retail industry by storm in the late 1980s and early 1990s, she created a new retail category—the cosmetics organizer category—with Caboodles' global retail sales exceeding US$100 million worldwide.

Ms. Mateer also works in the real estate industry, specializing in residential and lifestyle properties in New Zealand's winterless far north.

Her two daughters and four grandsons live in the United States and are a constant inspiration for many of her stories.

Other titles by Leonie Mateer:

Business:

The Caboodles Blueprint – Turn Your Idea into Millions

Have a Product Idea? – How Many Could You Sell? – a collection of business articles.

Health and wellbeing:

Psoriasis – The Simple Cure – Who Knew?

Psoriasis - Staying Clear - The Healthy Alternative – a must read for any psoriasis sufferer.

Fiction:

"The Audrey Murders" – a seven book series starring Audrey Wetherby, a serial killer living in idyllic small towns in New Zealand.

Children's fiction:

The Magical World of Dantonia

Black Lake

The Bird Boys

Mason's Secret

Tarot Card Online Game

www.readyourownfortune.com

A do-it-yourself game that enables players to read their own fortunes online, anytime, anywhere. Her sixty-three-card deck, based on ancient fortune telling cards, has been deciphered with the assistance of professional psychics.

www.ingramcontent.com/pod-product-compliance
Lightning Source LLC
Chambersburg PA
CBHW072052170626
46813CB00004B/1321

* 9 7 8 0 9 9 0 8 3 5 1 2 7 *